MEETING AGAIN

Before Jacinda could say a word, Ben opened the door to reveal Captain Morrow.

Her heart seemed to skip a beat at the sight of him. He looked handsome in his blue jacket, blue and white stripped waistcoat, and tan breeches with Hessians.

The captain stood for a moment in the doorway. He couldn't quite fathom that the beauty before him was once young Jack. Her golden hair had been styled into fashionable curls with a ribbon run through them. She looked elegant in a pale green traveling gown that showed her slender figure to perfection. The gown was trimmed with gold military-style frogging at the bodice, a ruff of gold lace inset at her collar. Tiny black leaves had been embroidered along the hem and at the ends of her sleeves. A straw casquet bonnet with small green flowers along the brim lay on the table beside her.

He took her hand and pressed a kiss on her glove. "My dear, you are too lovely for words."

BOOK YOUR PLACE ON OUR WEBSITE AND MAKE THE READING CONNECTION!

We've created a customized website just for our very special readers, where you can get the inside scoop on everything that's going on with Zebra, Pinnacle and Kensington books.

When you come online, you'll have the exciting opportunity to:

- View covers of upcoming books
- Read sample chapters
- Learn about our future publishing schedule (listed by publication month *and author*)
- Find out when your favorite authors will be visiting a city near you
- Search for and order backlist books from our online catalog
- Check out author bios and background information
- Send e-mail to your favorite authors
- Meet the Kensington staff online
- Join us in weekly chats with authors, readers and other guests
- Get writing guidelines
- AND MUCH MORE!

**Visit our website at
http://www.kensingtonbooks.com**

THE
CAPTAIN

LYNN COLLUM

ZEBRA BOOKS
Kensington Publishing Corp.
www.kensingtonbooks.com

PROLOGUE

Westbury, Somerset 1806

"What are you doin' here alone, Miss Jacinda?" The butler's snow-white brows drew together like a caterpillar who'd lost its way as he spied his young mistress sitting alone in the great hall.

"Cousin Millie is speaking with Papa, Stritch. He requested I wait here." The twelve-year-old gazed back at the old man with guileless innocence, never letting on that she'd just had her ear pressed to the library door for the mysterious meeting within. Something important was about to happen and Jacinda, like most children her age, had been curious. It was all about her.

The servant cocked his head as if he meant to question her but the front knocker sounded, staying his questions. Stritch opened the oversized door to find Baron Rowland and his heir, the Honorable Andrew Morrow, awaiting entry. It was rare that the local gentry visited Chettwood Manor due to Mr. Blanchett's unfortunate ties to trade, but the butler behaved in his normal, competent way.

His lordship strolled in with the confidence of a gentleman of title—no matter his straitened circumstances. At a glance one could see that a dissipated lifestyle had taken a toll on his once athletic physique and good looks. Thinning brown hair shot with gray was revealed when he handed his high crown beaver hat to Stritch. Heavy lines etched his eyes and mouth. His nose had grown red and bulbous from years of excess brandy and, more recently, the cheaper Blue Ruin. There was nothing stylish about him. His attire comprised a worn lawn shirt and a limp cravat, an unfashionable brown coat over a stripped green waistcoat sporting several stains, and battered brown buckskins long past their prime that met mud-caked boots with an obvious hole in one toe.

Pale gray eyes surveyed the interior of the great hall of Chettwood Manor with bored scrutiny, but within minutes of inspecting the opulent interior, there was a glimmer of interest in their cool depths. It was evident to the gentleman that Jacob Blanchett of B & B Foundry lived well—in truth, far better than Lord Rowland, a determined gamester.

For Jacinda, there was little awe at seeing the baron in her father's hallway. She was naively unaware of the power of such a man in light of his financial embarrassment. After one quick glance at him, she dismissed the baron as unimpressive. Of more interest was the son, a scant four years older than she.

The son, however, was different. Andrew Morrow's reputation preceded him. Jacinda owned a lively interest in the young man who'd wreaked havoc on the neighborhood for much of his life. He'd been a lively topic for gossip below stairs at most of the houses in the neighborhood, both grand and small. At Chettwood, Cook proclaimed that his wild ways were from boredom and Trudy vowed the cause must be neglect since the baron was often away, but Mr. Stritch had declared the young man a bad seed from a line of like gentlemen.

To Jacinda's youthful eyes, he seemed quite ordinary as he stood on their threshold. In no way did the young man resemble the devilish villain of gossip.

He hesitated a moment, staring at the butler, clearly reluctant to enter Chettwood's great hall. He lingered as if crossing the threshold would take him down a road from which there could be no return. Only after his father snapped at him to stop dawdling did he move to the gentleman's side where he stood as stiff as a fence post.

Her few memories of the young man were of a sullen figure in the back of the Morrow family pew. At present, he stood tall and lean, with an angular face that looked as if it had been chiseled from granite. It might have been deemed a handsome face if not for the grim set of his mouth. Sandy brown hair curled about his head in youthful disarray as if he'd failed to comb it that morning. There was a world-weary aspect to his dark green eyes, and a hint of sulkiness. Jacinda wondered just how much he knew of the plan that was being plotted at their expense—the plan she'd just overheard her father telling her governess.

As the young man turned to face his father, the full light of the hall's tall windows fell on him. Jacinda spied a small scar that ran from the edge of his right eye and arched down towards his cheek. Curiosity about the unusual mark grew. It was a strange, half-moon shape. On the face of a young man barely old enough to shave, it wasn't disfiguring or distracting, just something her sharp eyes noticed.

Then a strange thought entered her head. When she looked at him a peculiar feeling began in her stomach and it wasn't unpleasant. Would it really be so very bad to marry . . . someday? To be a baroness? To be mistress of her own establishment, like her dearly departed Mama had been. Then she remembered that her mother had always warned her never to marry without love: "*He must love you as you love him or there will be no wedded bliss.*" Jacinda was certain that all Papa's lady friends had made her mother very unhappy, though she didn't fully understand why.

Lord Rowland's gaze lit on Jacinda at that moment. "Is this the child?" There was shock in his voice but whether it was from her youth or from her frail appearance was unclear. She was well aware that the yellow gown Nurse had chosen made her pale cheeks look ghastly.

Stritch frowned and stiffly said, "This is Miss Blanchett, my lord." Jacinda rose and curtsied, but all the baron did was stare in his rude manner. Only Andrew Morrow acknowledged her with a stiff bow.

"I shall inform my master you have arrived, my lord." The butler hurried to the library to see whether Mr. Blanchett would receive visitors.

Jacinda sat down and tugged her ugly black shawl tighter round her frail shoulders as the young man's proud gaze rested on her. Outrage registered on his face and he moved closer to his father to whisper, but anger made his voice carry in the large room. "I tell you, Father, a marriage contract with a compete stranger is monstrously unfair, sir. She's little more than a baby. Besides, you have always said Blanchett smells of the shop."

Lowering his own voice, the baron shushed the boy. "You'll do your duty." He, too, stared at the Jacinda. "Why, only look at her. It ain't likely the chit will see her eighteenth birthday. Why should we not take advantage of the cit's offer? Besides, the mother was quality. Viscount Devere is her uncle, though there's little enough money there—which is why the woman was married off to Blanchett. He's made it plain that we get part of the funds up front *and* a guarantee that if she don't survive we still get the remainder of the settlement. The man's even promised there will be no need for restitution if the marriage don't take place due to death or her refusal once she's of age. All we need do is trust time and bitter winters will rescue you from having to fulfill the pledge."

A bubble of hysterical laughter welled up in Jacinda. Her father and Lord Rowland each thought they had the upper hand in this dreadful arrangement. Yet neither cared about her feelings. She was no better than one of the little marble pawns on Papa's chess table.

Before any sound escaped her lips, she was able to tamp down the outburst when she saw the flash of pity in Andrew's eyes as they raked her a second time. It was the one thing she hated most and saw it too often in the faces of the Quality in the neighborhood. She lifted her chin and stared back at him defiantly. Everyone thought her weak and unworthy, but she would show them all one day.

Unswayed by the baron's argument, Andrew Morrow protested, "Father, I have loved Miss Amberly since making her acquaintance two years ago. I warn you, if you enter this betrothal on my behalf, I shall do something drastic." His voice broke and dropped lower. A red stain flushed his cheeks, causing the white scar to stand out.

The baron grabbed his son's lapels and pulled him close. "You'll do as you're told, boy. Squire Amberly knows he has a diamond of the first water. He won't squander her beauty on a penniless peer's son. Remember, Rowland Park is mortgaged to the hilt and if you want to have a home, I must pay off some of the mortgages."

Before the young man could respond, Stritch quietly returned and cleared his throat. Rowland released his son at the sound. "My lord, Mr. Blanchett will see you in the library."

The baron pointed at a chair on the opposite side of the occasional table from where Jacinda sat. "Stay here. I won't allow you to ruin this opportunity. I'll summon you if you are needed."

Son glared at father for a moment as if he meant to defy him, then with a shrug he stalked to the chair and threw himself into the seat so hard that the legs scraped the marble floor. He slumped dejectedly, his gaze riveted on the black and white tiles. The baron marched down the hall and passed into the library without a backward glance. The butler closed the door and departed after giving a warning glance to the young mistress.

Jacinda surveyed the young man with curiosity from hooded eyes. It was rather like watching a pot slowly come to a boil. He began to wring his hands and shift his feet as a muscle twitched in his jaw. Realizing he was under scrutiny, he turned his gaze on her as if she were some vile thing that had slithered in from the lake.

"It's rude to stare, girl."

"I'm not staring and my name is Jacinda, not girl." Angry at his tone, she stuck her tongue out.

He rolled his eyes. "Brat!"

"Toad!"

"Baby!"

"Bad seed!"

With another roll of his eyes, he turned his head and

hunched lower in the seat, his gaze locked straight ahead. A footman came from below stairs carrying a bottle of brandy. He entered the library and soon returned, but before the door closed the sound of the baron's laughter penetrated the hall.

On hearing his father, Andrew Morrow darted to his feet and muttered, "I'll kill him before I'll give up Mariah."

Without another word, he crossed the hall, jerked open the front door, and left.

It was apparent her future husband had taken her in aversion. Who could blame him? She was decidedly plain. Her hair was that indeterminate color between brown and blonde and hung in lank waves to her waist. Her hazel eyes were perhaps the only flattering feature on her ordinary face. The delicate little mole at the corner of her mouth, which her mother had called a beauty mark, was the cause of the degrading nickname, "Spot," that her cousin, Giles, had given her. His sister, Prudence, never used it but always laughed when her brother used the horrid name.

Still glumly contemplating Andrew Morrow's abrupt departure, she started when the front door opened and her resident tormentors, fresh from their morning ride, came noisily into the great hall. Jacinda sat back in her chair in the silent hope her cousins would pass through into the breakfast parlor without seeing her. But clearly her luck was out that morning.

Giles Devere dropped his crop and gloves on a table near the door, then swept off his hat and tossed it upon a chair. At one-and-twenty he was already showing signs of the plumpness that had plagued his late father. His golden blond hair had been brushed into a neat Brutus and his beaver hat had done little to crush the elegance of the creation. "I tell you it was Andrew Morrow who almost ran us down. He always was one to ride as if the devil were on his heels."

Prudence Devere, six years her brother's junior and as thin as her brother was plump, followed suit and tossed her gear beside his. A grin split her lightly freckled face, the unfortunate result of too much sun on a redhead's fair skin. "Guess he found out that Mariah Amberly drove out with Chesterfield's heir yesterday." A girlish giggle punctuated the remark.

Giles caught sight of Jacinda and frowned. "What are you doing out of your cotton wool, Spot? You are determined to make us your father's heirs by your reckless behavior—or so your governess would have the world believe."

Jacinda realized he was being facetious; the Deveres were, in fact, her Mama's relatives. Her father had allowed his wife to invite them to stay after a tearful plea from Mrs. Devere that they were destitute and Viscount Devere had offered them no help.

"I'm not sick. There is no reason I cannot come down to the hall." Jacinda resisted the urge to again stick out her tongue at Giles. He did seem to bring out the worst in her.

Prudence sighed, "Nonsense, you are always sick. Miss Markham just hasn't determined what it is yet . . . but take heart, I'm sure she will pronounce you ailing with something by the end of the day."

The two siblings laughed and headed for their breakfast without inviting their young cousin to join them. Jacinda sighed. They were right. Cousin Millie, who acted as her governess, saw danger for her charge everywhere. It was unfortunate that Jacinda's young brother had not survived his birth. She would then have not been the entire focus of Millie's attention. Jacinda slumped back in her chair and stared out the window. She wondered what was happening behind the library door. What was to be her fate?

The green baize door to the servants' hall swung open some five minutes later and her father's new steward, Mr. Weems, strode into the great hall from below stairs. Welsh, his auburn good looks always set the maids to chattering about him when he came to speak with Mr. Blanchett. He'd been at Chettwood a scant three months, but already he'd improved the estate, or so Mr. Blanchett had claimed when several of the tenants complained about the changes the young steward had instituted.

"Good morning, is Miss Markham about? She asked to have a word with me this morning."

"She is engaged with Papa at the moment but—"

Before she could finish, the lady in question marched out of the library, her gaunt face flushed an angry red and her lace cap askew. "Come, Jacinda. 'Tis time you had your rest. It seems *my* wishes will be ignored and you must go with your father to Rowland Park this evening." She grabbed her young relative's arm and started for the stairs when her gaze fell on the steward, who stood unobtrusively against the wall. "Oh, Weems, forgive me, but I am too distracted with all this talk of Jacinda's betrothal to plan the enclosing of the summer house beside the lake."

"Marriage for the little one?" Shock reflected on the steward's handsome face as he looked to Jacinda.

"Appalling, is it not?" Millicent said over her shoulder as she pulled her young charge up the stairs.

Jacinda looked back at Weems, who appeared perplexed for a moment as he watched them. Then he turned to the open library door to stare at the two gentlemen huddled over her father's desk. It seemed every adult but her father and the baron deemed this betrothal improper.

Cousin Millie led Jacinda up to her rooms and left her with Nurse. She gave instructions for the child to be dressed and ready in her best gown by six o'clock sharp. After the lady departed, the servant bustled about, turning back the covers on the large four-post bed. "What's got Miss Millie in such a takin', miss?"

Jacinda wasn't sleepy in the least, but she dutifully allowed Nurse to undo the ties to her gown, then she kicked off her slippers and climbed in. With complete childhood innocence, she announced to the woman, who was scarcely ten years older than she, "It seems I'm betrothed, Trudy."

Nurse's hand froze in the act of covering the young girl she had taken to her heart after the death of the child's mother. "What nonsense, miss! Ye is still a babe."

"It shall be a long betrothal. Papa has arranged it with Lord Rowland."

The servant tucked her in, then settled into a nearby chair, shaking her head. "I'll never understand the ways of Quality. Pledging children to wed, upon my word."

Jacinda nestled down into the pillows and stared up at the angels Cousin Millie had had painted on the ceiling to watch over her. "His lordship's son doesn't want to marry me."

Trudy's brows drew together as she picked up her darning. "Why, he'd be lucky to have the likes of ye, Miss Jacinda. A future baron he may be, but it's well known throughout the county that there's bad blood there. His lordship is a loose screw for certain. But never ye mind his slight, his son's just a lad and don't know what he wants, child."

Jacinda chuckled at how incensed Nurse sounded. "Oh, I'm not the least offended he doesn't wish to marry me. He's in love with Miss Mariah Amberly."

A dawning look settled on Nurse's plain features. "He and the rest of the neighborhood sprigs. Close those eyes, child, and get some rest."

Jacinda tried to sleep, but her mind was too full of Nurse's words. Bad blood in the Morrows. What could Papa be thinking? Then she remembered Andrew's last utterance. He'd threatened to kill someone. Who did he mean? She knew him so little and wondered if he had such wickedness within. Nurse seemed to think so and, in Jacinda's opinion, who knew better about such things than Trudy, whose own brother was a bloodthirsty villain. Well, actually he was just a highwayman, but still, she would know about such things, would she not?

The girl's thoughts settled on that man who had grown into a dashing figure in her imagination. She opened her eyes and gazed at Nurse, who sat stitching away at something black and shapeless. "Have you heard from Johnny?"

The servant's brown gaze flew to her charge. "Never ye mind about me brother. Go to sleep, child."

Jacinda scooted higher on the pillows. "I would never tell a single soul about him. Is he in Somerset?"

Nurse glanced at the door as if fearful someone would hear her. "Aye, he's back. I keep urgin' him to find an honest livin' here, but he swears he's no longer workin' the Pike. He's a good man but I worry so for him and his wanderlust. He's a son of his own, so it's high time he settled down at his age."

"A son?"

"Aye, little Ben." Nurse's face grew soft at the thought of her nephew. "His mother worked at The King's Arms and lives with the boy near Bristol. Johnny comes to visit regular and is always full of promises."

A shiver of excitement raced through Jacinda. With all the innocence of youth, she still believed such a life was full of adventure, ignoring the danger. "Can I meet him next time he comes?"

"Not as long as I draw breath. Go to sleep, Miss Jacinda."

The girl well knew that tone. She would get nothing else from Nurse. She snuggled down into the covers and soon fell asleep, despite her apprehension about what lay ahead.

Apollo's hooves pounded the hard gravel road rhythmically as Andrew pressed him to lengthen his stride. He wanted to be far away from his father and that sickly child they were trying to foist on him. In heated anger, he passed several riders along the road but who they were he couldn't say, so deep was his grievance against his sire.

Perhaps the worst part was that if this settlement were signed, within six months the baron would be right back where he was at the moment—in need of funds. Only then, Andrew would be obliged to marry that plain child at the time and place of their fathers' choosing.

He reined his horse to a walk and stared out at the green valley he loved. In the distance to the south, he could see the villages of Westbury and Wookey where he'd spent so much time. This was his home and had been for generations of his family before him. He'd always thought that he would live, marry, produce his heir, and die here. Had his father robbed him of his legacy with his excessive gaming?

At the thought of his own marriage, his father's warning echoed in his head. Would Squire Amberly really refuse to allow him to pay his addresses to Mariah? A flash of memory from the spring Horse Fair filled his mind. The old squire had followed behind Lord Chesterfield, one of the wealthiest landowners in this part of the county, and behaved like the man's servant instead of a country gentleman.

An overwhelming desire to see Mariah rose in him. He would not be denied his true love by his father or hers. He would elope, take her to Gretna and marry over the anvil. But as that image seeped into his brain, his lip curled in distaste. Perhaps it was his age that made him see life as black and white and such a shoddy, scandalous marriage was not for him and his Mariah. Besides, he hadn't enough money to hire a carriage and horses, much less to pay for inns and marriage.

A wave of despair washed over Andrew and he sagged in the saddle, a gesture his horse interpreted as a signal to stop. The lad sat in the middle of the road, his dark thoughts gripping him. His father was right. Mariah wouldn't be allowed to marry him, and the very thought made him ill. A title would not be enough to sway the squire. There were easily five men in the neighborhood with fortunes and titles. Squire Amberly would never allow Andrew near her with his pockets to let.

Pain radiated through his chest as that truth struck him hard. He ground his teeth in frustration. But his youth helped him to rally and he soon determined there had to be a way. He must have funds before he could present himself as Miss Amberly's suitor. Not just funds, but a fortune of his own since his father was like a giant hole in the ground that sucked up every cent that came within his reach.

Andrew's eyes narrowed as he put his mind to the problem. How did an English gentleman make money except from his land? The very thought of trade made a chill race over him. Nothing would put a period to his hopes with Mariah more than to have her father discover that the future Lord Rowland had soiled his hands in such a manner.

His gaze drifted west toward Bristol Channel, some fifteen miles away. He remembered his last trip to the coast before his mother had died, when he'd sat and watched white sails of ships going about their business. He'd longed to experience great adventure back then, but everything had changed. His eyes widened as an idea took root. There was only one way to avoid this betrothal *and* earn the funds he needed. He would have to leave.

Where did everyone go to get rich? *India!* His hands tightened on the reins. That was it, he would go to India and make his fortune. For the first time that day, a smile tipped his mouth.

But first he must secure Mariah's pledge to wait for him. She must know that he would do all this for her. Full of romantic notions and convinced that he had come up with the perfect solution to his dilemma, he set off for Amberly Court, determined to have a private conversation with his beloved.

Despite the day's excitement, Jacinda slept soundly. Trudy shook her awake just after five. She was quickly dressed in her blue velvet gown with a white lace collar that Aunt Devere had brought back from London last fall. Jacinda's hair was brushed and tied with a matching blue ribbon. She wore the gold locket with two entwined ruby hearts that had once belonged to her mother. It always made her feel as if her mother were watching over her. One glance in the mirror and she knew that the fussy gown did little to improve her looks and that the locket was overlarge for her frail frame. As usual, a gaunt, pale ghost of a child looked back from her glass.

At six o'clock sharp Trudy led Jacinda down to the great hall, where Cousin Millie was in a heated argument with Mr. Blanchett. The gentleman was elegantly dressed in evening attire, and his brown hair, shot with red highlights, was neatly groomed and gleaming in the candlelight. A riding accident that very week had forced him to use a gold-topped cane, but he'd declared it made him look more the fashionable swell, which always seemed important to the foundry-owner-turned-country-gentleman. To Jacinda's eyes he was quite a handsome man, even at fifty.

Aunt Devere, all blond curls and rouged cheeks, was off to one side, listening but not voicing her opinion one way or the other. The widow rarely disagreed with her late sister-in-law's husband. She would only face his wrath when it came to pleading for him to increase her son's allowances or begging him to be lenient when Giles had engaged in some folly that displeased Mr. Blanchett. Otherwise, she had little to say to him.

"Enough!" Blanchett roared at last. "I'll not have you ruining the evening with your sour face and attitude, Millie. You shan't go." He turned to Mrs. Devere, who turned her back to the gentleman's and gave a shake of her head. He shrugged, then looked at Nurse. "What is your name?"

The young servant quaked, but she curtsied. "Trudeau, sir. Aggie Trudeau."

"You're old Ben's daughter?" When the girl acknowledged her father had been the gentleman's head groom
before his death, Mr. Blanchett nodded his approval.
"Your father was a good man. Well, Trudeau, you will
be Jacinda's companion this evening. Go find a wrap."

Without a word, Nurse hurried up the stairs even as
Millicent Markham began a new round of haranguing
the gentleman. "This is beyond foolish, sir. The child
has only just recovered from an inflamation of the lungs
and you intend to take her out into the night chill."

He searched his daughter's gaunt face and saw nothing worrisome. "That was two months ago, and she will
never regain her strength locked forever in her rooms.
She looks fit to me; therefore, she shall go." His tone
brooked no further argument, even from Millicent.

They stood in strained silence until Nurse returned,
then Mr. Blanchett softened his attitude, turning on his
charm. "Take heart, Millie. We won't be late. I shall have
Jacinda home before eleven, I promise. Then you may
cosset her to your heart's content."

The lady's lips pressed together in a grim line and
she made no comment other than to remind her niece
to heed her manners. In frosty silence, the spinster
marched up the stairs in a huff.

Millie's display of pique did little to deter Mr.
Blanchett. He ushered his daughter outside with Nurse
on their heels. Her father directed that a small leather-
bound chest be put in the carriage. The trio climbed into
the large family coach and traveled the five miles to
Rowland Park, which lay beyond the small village of
Wookey. All the while her father kept telling her that
one day she would be thankful for what he was doing.

The only thing of note about the evening was Andrew
Morrow's absence. His father made excuses about a

prior engagement, but even Jacinda's father seemed skeptical. For Jacinda it was simply an excessively long, boring night with bad food and no real company while the gentlemen retired to the library to transact their business.

At nine o'clock, Jacob Blanchett insisted he must take his daughter home for it was well past her bedtime.

Lord Rowland grinned, his red-shot gaze settling on the girl. "Ah, yes, we wouldn't want anything to happen to our future baroness, now would we?"

A chill raced down Jacinda's spine. She understood that was exactly what he and his son did hope. She pulled her shawl tighter round her shoulders and looked to her father, but he seemed to see nothing wrong in the baron's words.

Trudy was summoned along with the carriage, and they set out for home. Mr. Blanchett settled back into the squabs, greatly satisfied with the night's work. They rode in silence for much of the way before her father spoke. "You are destined to be Baroness Rowland one day, my dear. Never forget that. The baron might think he can wiggle out of our agreement, but the paperwork he signed tonight will go to my solicitor in the morning post, just in case."

There was something in her father's voice that frightened Jacinda. "In case of what, Papa?"

He stared at her in the dim light of the carriage. Jacinda had always sensed his disappointment that she was not as pretty as her mother. Her father liked pretty women and she was not.

"Perhaps it's nothing, but even though I chose to allow my brother to run the Foundry and retired to a gentleman's life in the country, I'm not an utter fool. Everyone thinks I—"

A pistol discharged in the nearby darkness. A shouted "Stand and deliver" penetrated the closed carriage. Mr. Blanchett moved to lower the window and look out. To Jacinda's surprise, the coachman disobeyed the barked demand. The crack of a whip sounded and the carriage began to sway back and forth as the horses thundered forward.

"Papa, what is happening?" Jacinda grabbed at her father's hand.

He didn't answer her. Instead, he spoke to Nurse. "Trudeau, if they get the carriage stopped, protect the child with your life."

"Yes, sir." Nurse's tone was surprisingly brave to Jacinda's ears.

The dark shadows of the countryside flashed by the windows as they fled from the highwaymen. Jacinda had never ridden so fast and the sharp sway of the carriage made her feel queasy. Another shot rang out and a strange thud sounded above them.

"They've shot the coachman."

Jacinda recognized the concern in her father's voice. The carriage began to sway from one side of the road to the other as the horses sensed the loss of control. Mr. Blanchett swore under his breath as they were thrown about inside the small space. The swaying grew more pronounced and her father shouted, "Brace yourself, I think we're going to crash."

Jacinda flew forward as the sound of cracking wood and breaking glass filled the air. The air was knocked from her and for a moment she couldn't breathe.

A strange stillness filled the carriage. Stunned, it took several minutes before Jacinda's senses registered that the vehicle was no longer moving. The carriage lay at an angle against a boulder. In the darkness she could hear the groans of her father and Trudy as well as the distant sound of their team hurling away, still harnessed to the broken shaft.

"Papa?" Jacinda reached out for her father but he was already climbing out the door, now positioned over their heads.

"Hurry!" he called as he jumped to the ground and grabbed her hand. Roughly, he pulled her from the wreckage. Minutes later Trudy stood beside her. The sound of riders approaching made her father cry, "Take my daughter up into those rocks."

"Aye, sir." Trudy clamped a hand over Jacinda's arm and dragged her across the road. Jacinda looked back to see the dark shape of her father standing in the moonlight, leaning heavily on the cane he'd salvaged from the wreck as he stared in the direction of the highwaymen.

"Papa? Are you not coming?"

"Not a word, child, and don't come out until Trudeau says its safe."

The two females scrambled up through the rocks and found a large boulder that jutted out. Trudy pulled the child down into the circle of her arms, and whispered, "Not a peep, Miss Jacinda, no matter what you hear."

Jacinda nodded her head. What was going to happen to them? Why had those men chased them? In the darkness she couldn't tell how close they were to home. She had never wanted to see Cousin Millie as much as she did at that very moment.

The horses thundered up. A gunshot exploded in the darkness. Both girls flinched at the report. Trudy leaned forward to peer round the rock's edge, then gasped and drew back. She whimpered and prayed, "Oh, sweet Lord protect us!"

Jacinda strained her ears for her father's voice but all

she heard was the gravelly rasp of the highwayman's question. "Is he dead?"

Jacinda bit her lip to keep from screaming and tears welled in her eyes. They had shot Papa.

"Not yet, but it won't be long," a second voice answered. "'E's got a nice plump purse."

"Stubble it and find the child. We ain't done until we take care of the child."

The air froze in Jacinda's lungs even as Trudy's arms tightened protectively. They wanted her. Why? She had no money. Her fingers suddenly clamped over her mother's locket. She prayed they wouldn't take that from her.

Footsteps sounded on the wrecked carriage then a voice called, "She ain't 'ere."

"Search the area. Ain't no pay unless we finish the job."

For the next few minutes Trudy and Jacinda lay in their hiding place holding their breath as the two brigands roved over the rocks across the road where the wrecked carriage lay. They had just reached the base of the hill on the other side of the road when the leader stopped. He swore loudly, then shouted, "Someone's coming. We'll 'ave to get the brat later."

Within minutes, sounds of the horses galloping away filled the night. Jacinda shoved Trudy's arms aside and scrambled down the hill to her father. The servant protested, but followed her charge back to the roadway. Jacinda fell to her knees while Trudy stood and peered into the darkness in the direction the highwaymen had ridden. In the opposite distance the jangle of a slow-moving vehicle rattled.

"Papa, Papa." Jacinda grabbed her father's coat, tears streaming down her cheeks.

A weak hand came up to grab her wrist. "Where— where . . . is . . . your nurse?"

Trudy came to his other side. "Here, sir."

"Trudeau," Mr. Blanchett coughed, and they could hear a strange rattle as he breathed. "Listen to me. You must leave Somerset and take Jacinda with you."

"Leave, Papa, no! I won't go without you." Tears rolled unchecked, dropping on her hands as they clutched at her father as if she could hold on for him.

"Hush, child. This is too important. Trudeau . . . did you hear those men?"

"Aye, sir, I did. They was wantin' to hurt Miss Jacinda."

"No, to kill her. You must protect her." Jacinda openly sobbed at her father's words, but he continued, knowing his time was running out. "Make certain my solicitor gets these documents." He was scarcely able to lift the leather pouch and his hand fell limply to the ground once the servant had taken the papers. "I am asking a great deal, but in the end my daughter will reward you, Trudeau. Take the diamond stick pin in my cravat and whatever else I have and sell it. That should keep you in funds until perhaps the truth will be revealed about this night's evil work. Don't trust anyone, girl. Not my family or my friends. Protect her until she's old enough to recognize the danger. When you send the documents, have Jacinda write a letter to my solicitor, Thomas Wilkins, in London. She's to inform him that only when you deem it's safe, she will return to claim her rightful heritage. Make certain she never tells him her location. He would be duty-bound to return her to Chettwood."

Jacob Blanchett took another rattling breath, then tightened his grip on his daughter's arm. "Jacinda, my dearest child, things are going to be difficult for you, but you must be strong. Do as Trudeau tells you. Always remember that someone wants my fortune and that they are willing to kill you to get it. I—I'm sorry, my dear. I have . . . have done many things I regret. I should have done something sooner when . . . when I . . . began to suspect a . . . danger . . . after . . . my riding acc— accident. I love . . . you. . . ." there was a soft rush of air, then the gentleman fell silent. His hand dropped from her.

Jacinda fell prostrate over her father's body and wept bitterly but Trudy turned in the direction of the approaching vehicle. The servant peered into the darkness at the light from the carriage lantern that flickered in the distance. She straightened as if coming to some decision. She leaned over and grabbed the child's arm. "Hurry, Miss Jacinda, someone's comin' and if we don't leave now, I won't be able to follow your father's directions."

"But, I—I don't want to go and leave P-Papa."

The little servant knelt on the ground. "Miss—" Trudy stopped. It would never do to still be so formal while they were on the run. "Jacinda, yer life is in danger and yer papa is no longer here to protect ye. He's given that task to me and I intend to make certain ye are safe." Trudy grimly fumbled on the blood-soaked chest of her late employer until she found the diamond stick pin. She pulled it from the cravat and stowed it in her pocket. She hesitated a moment, then pulled the gold watch from his waistcoat and the large gold ring his wore on his hand and put them with the pin. She would need these items and more to support the child until Jacinda was old enough to take care of herself. Trudy stood and pulled the weeping child up with her.

"W-Where will we go?" Jacinda's whole world had

shattered. She couldn't even begin to think about life without her father.

"We are going to find my brother, Johnny. He will know how we can survive this. Ye must be brave, child."

"I'm not afraid of him."

"Who child?" Nurse was puzzled at the child's sudden calm.

"Andrew Morrow. He and his father did this."

"We don't know that child. We'll leave such matters to your father's solicitor. He'll find out who hired those men."

But Jacinda remembered the young man's angry words . . . and now her father was dead. There was no doubt in her heart.

At the moment the carriage rounded the bend, two females slipped into the dark woods near the rocks and disappeared. All the local merchant and his fat wife returning from market day in Wells found was a wrecked coach with the body of Mr. Blanchett in the road.

CHAPTER ONE

London, 1814

"Wake up, sir." Mr. James Wormwood's clerk shook his shoulder on finding him fast asleep, hunched over his desk. It was a common state for Mr. Elliot to find his employer in of late, which accounted for the fact that Wormwood and Styles, Solicitors, had lost a great many of their clients in the past year. At the age of sixty-five, the senior partner was ready to retire but unfortunately lacked the funds.

"Sir . . . sir, there's a gentleman to see you."

The solicitor opened his eyes and asked, "Who is it? If it's Mackleby again, tell him I ain't in." He closed his eyes as if he meant to return to sleep.

"It's a new gentleman, sir, and I think he's someone of importance."

Mr. Wormwood lifted his head and smoothed his thinning gray hair. "Dressed to the nines, is he?"

"Well, no, sir."

The old solicitor took a long swig from a cup that was full of spirits and a little coffee. "Dripping in jewelry, is he?"

"Not even a single fob, sir."

Wormwood looked at his clerk, his brushy gray brows

drawn together. "Have you been nipping from my cup, Ned?"

Shock reflected on Mr. Elliot's face. "Not a bit of it, sir."

"Then how the devil do you know the man's of some importance?" Mr. Wormwood slid his glasses on and peered at his now frightened employee.

"His name, sir. It's Morrow. 'Tis the family name of Baron Rowland, is it not?"

The solicitor frowned. "Can't be. Rowland's heir ran off years ago. It was quite a scandal in Somerset at the time. Lad was only sixteen or so as I remember. The baron gave him up for dead."

"That's as may be, Mr. Wormwood, but the gentleman introduced himself as Captain Drew Morrow and he's wishin' to speak with you on a matter of some importance."

The old man sat back in his worn leather chair, his face full of surprise. "I do believe the boy was called Andrew. Can it be the same?" The solicitor gestured at the clerk to hurry. "Stop your dawdling, man, and send him in."

The clerk opened his mouth to protest, then decided it was pointless and hurried out. Minutes later a tall, lean gentleman with darkly tanned skin stepped into the room. The visitor was not fashionably attired, but he wore his clothes with an easy assurance of self that defied fashion. His dark hair was longer than the current fashion. It brushed the top of his shoulders, the ends sun-streaked blond. Yet the thing that struck the old gentleman the most was the distinctive half-moon scar that arched down from the man's right eye. Wormwood had asked about it once while staying at Rowland Park. He'd been told it was a childhood burn the boy had acquired while the farriers had been shoeing a horse. This *was* his lordship's long lost son.

Wormwood rose rather unsteadily and extended his hand. "Why, it is you, sir. You were scarcely more than a lad the last time I was at Rowland Park. Elliot tells me you are Captain Morrow these days. Well done!"

A half-smile exposed teeth that gleamed brightly in contrast to the man's tan cheeks. "I was hoping you would remember me, sir. I have come desiring information about my father."

Mr. Wormwood gestured toward a seat. After both gentlemen were settled, the old man stared across at the face that he was certain women would find handsome. *Ah, to be young and appealing again* . . . but he put the thought aside and asked, "After all these years, what prompted you to inquire? Why not write the baron directly or better yet, pay him a visit?"

Drew Morrow fidgeted uncomfortably in the worn chair. The solicitor was so altered he almost hadn't recognized him. Had his father changed so much as well? The young captain pondered the old gentleman's questions. He'd been such a fool all those years ago, and it was always difficult to put one's actions into words for they seemed all the more foolish. He wasn't sure he could make Wormwood understand. Drew had a need to reconnect with his roots but was uncertain that Lord Rowland would wish his return. Truth be told, Drew wasn't even sure he understood himself. Perhaps it was the emptiness of life at sea or merely the passage of time that had matured him. More likely it was a sense of his own mortality. All he was certain about was a desire to heal the rift he had opened eight years earlier by his flight in the face of adversity. He needed to do this.

He leaned back and sighed. "I should have done so sooner, sir. But"—he shrugged—"the first few years after I left were spent just learning to survive." A sheepish grin touched his lips. "Besides, I was very much piqued at my father for all his plots and plans back then." He watched a moth fluttering near the window seeking to escape the overwarm room. "There was also a part of me that feared he would come for me and make me return home to fulfill his wishes. I was quite determined that wasn't going to happen." The captain grew pensive but didn't dwell on those times. "Pride in a young man is a rather powerful thing, sir."

The old solicitor merely nodded, for he had much experience dealing with young sprigs come to Town to make their mark and very often failing. He remained silent—his cue that he would listen.

Drew's gaze moved past the old gentleman's shoulder to a badly rendered painting of country life. "As my luck turned, I felt like it would appear to be gloating if I wrote him. The more time passed, the harder it became. I picked up a pen a thousand times, but told myself that he wouldn't want to hear from a disloyal son who'd foiled all his plans." He fell silent and his eyes took on a faraway look for a moment before he continued. "Then, about six months ago in the throes of a typhoon off the China coast, I came rather close to death. The narrow escape made me take stock of what I thought important, about what I wanted to accomplish. It was something of a revelation when I realized that I had a duty to my name as well as to my father. I am his sole heir. I promised myself I would come back and make amends for abandoning him when he needed my help. I've made my fortune and can do much to help make Rowland Park once again profitable. That is, if he still acknowledges me. I am well aware the estate is not entailed."

Mr. Wormwood's brown eyes brightened on hearing the word fortune. "You must know that I shall be delighted to represent you in any way I can. As to the old gentleman, he remarried, oh, three years ago. Perhaps to try for another heir, or to acquire the widow's portion, but"—the old man shrugged—"all he obtained was a young wife"—the solicitor's mouth twisted with distaste—"who has no more head for money than the baron. Within a year they were dished again, but he'd staved off the most pressing of the creditors. I have no doubt he would welcome you home."

His father with a new wife! Drew was unable to stop the surprise from registering on his face. Despite the man's penchant for gaming, he'd had a strong sense of the continuity of family. Yet, he'd stoutly refused to wed while Drew had been a young man, saying all he needed was one heir. Had his father given up on ever seeing his only son alive again? A wave of guilt washed over Drew. He had much to make up for where that gentleman was concerned. "Then my father is well?"

"Up until about six months ago." The solicitor shook his head sadly.

Drew's hand tightened on the arm of the chair. "He is alive, is he not?"

"Alive, but he was injured in a riding accident during a hunt. Happened just before Twelfth Night. He's been confined to his bed since. The physician can find nothing wrong. But your father's will to walk seems lacking. I've done what I can to help, but I fear I had little to work with, what with the estate so mortgaged. The rumors after the murder only complicated things and—"

Captain Morrow straightened. "What murder, sir?"

A dawning light flashed in the solicitor tired eyes. "I had forgotten, all that happened about the time you left. In fact, your father told me you vanished the same night of the murder." He quickly explained about Mr. Blanchett's violent death, Miss Blanchett's flight along with her maid, and the rumors that eventually surfaced that the baron or his son might have been involved. "But, of course, that was utter nonsense, sir, as you well know. When the child went missing, Mr. Wilkins, Blanchett's solicitor, refused to pay another penny against the betrothal agreement, as there was no thought that a marriage could take place without her or you for that matter."

"Are you telling me that there are people in Somerset who actually think I might have killed that man?" Shock paled the captain's face.

Mr. Wormwood pulled a linen handkerchief from a drawer, then took off his spectacles and began to clean them. "Your reputation, if memory serves, was likely the cause, my boy. But that was long ago. No doubt other theories have surfaced since, for there is the matter of the child's fortune. Plenty of relations in her family could have had a hand in what happened. The old man might have been an infamous philanderer, but he was no fool when he ordered her maid to take her into hiding."

"Philandering?" Drew vaguely remembered he'd heard rumors about the cit even as a young man. "Might that have been a cause of the attack? A jealous husband, an irate father?"

"Not likely, since the child wrote her father's solicitor

that the killers searched the rocks to find her as well. As to by-blows, Wilkins swears that Blanchett financially provided for his"—the old lawyer's cheeks reddened— "er, mistakes, as I prefer to call them, which is better than most gentlemen to the manor born."

The captain rose and moved to stand in front of the fireplace. He stared at the cold ashes in the fireplace, his hands clasped behind him. He'd come seeking information about a father who'd shown little interest in him except as a bargaining tool. Yet, Drew had come to realize that blood bound them no matter how one tried to ignore such. Still, he was unprepared for what the solicitor had related. The very man his father had dealings with had died the night Drew fled. Was it mere coincidence? Or was his father in some way involved? The thought sent a chill down his spine, but he dismissed the idea at once. Rowland had proven himself a man of honor by not fleeing to the continent when his debts had grown so large. Surely such a man wouldn't stoop to murder when he'd had the settlement money within his grasp.

Regardless, the feeling that he and his father were to blame settled over Drew like a cloud on a summer day. The proposed marriage might have been the trigger for Blanchett's murder, which made it inevitable that he and his father would come under suspicion. It made no sense for them to have killed the very man who would have solved their problems, but very often such rumors were spread maliciously for no good reason.

Drew searched his memory for an image of Mr. Blanchett, but the cit hadn't mixed much in local society and Drew knew him more from reputation than through personal contact. A man like that was always a popular subject in a small village. Blanchett had liked the ladies, though, for his name had often been linked to this widow or that light skirt. But as a wealthy widower with only one child, most likely it was as Wormwood had suggested: that the murderer was someone after the child's portion. Blanchett had smelled of trade, but he had married a viscount's daughter in his quest to improve his situation. His daughter was the key to the mystery.

Drew look back over his shoulder and saw his father's solicitor watching him in silent speculation. It was a look he would have to get used to if he returned home, for in Somerset many might still wonder about his and his father's involvement. He returned to his seat, a determined set to his jaw. "You say they never found the girl, er . . ." he struggled to remember her name, but all he could come up with was "Miss Blanchett." Why, she had scarcely been more than a baby when he'd seen her at Chettwood Manor that fateful day. The hazy image of a plain, pale child with overlarge eyes drifted at the edges of his memory. A brat who'd given him tit for tat, as he recalled.

"Never, but Mr. Wilkins, Blanchett's solicitor, swears the girl's still alive. Been in communication with her. At least, he receives the occasional letter, albeit she never discloses her location. Says she will only come back once the murderer is brought to justice." Wormwood shrugged. "After all these years, I daresay that isn't likely to happen. The only thing that would protect the girl would be for her to marry and have a house full of heirs."

A cold sensation coiled in Drew's stomach. Had his father set this disaster in motion? Had he helped by running out on the child bride he didn't want? He'd been such a romantic fool back then. The image of the beautiful Mariah Amberly surfaced. A memory stirred in him as he thought about his righteous indignation at being asked to sacrifice his true love to save Rowland Park from creditors. . . .

Drew hadn't thought of her in years. Her beauty and his youth had blinded him to her fickle and shallow nature. He'd been in Calcutta scarcely a year and all but starving when he'd seen her wedding announcement to a wealthy earl thrice her age in an old copy of the London Times. Looking back through the years, he could see that what he'd felt for her was infatuation, but still, her abandonment had wounded his youthful heart. Time had taught him that females were mercenary creatures in general. Like most of her kind, Mariah had chosen money over love.

A bevy of beauties had passed through his life and his bed since, yet not one had touched his heart. Or perhaps he'd kept them from doing so, knowing they would only use him as Mariah had. What was more important to him was that frail Blanchett girl—he froze. "Mr. Wormwood, did my father sign the betrothal agreement with Blanchett?"

"Aye, he did. Sent me his copy of the document." The old man rose and went to a cabinet and pulled out a drawer, taking little note of the grim set of his visitor's face. Wormwood rummaged through the clutter for several minutes before he found the wanted document. "Blanchett made one advance payment the night they signed the papers. The rest was to be transferred into your father's account once Mr. Wilkins received the documents, but like I said, that never happened."

Drew took the papers the solicitor handed him. He quickly perused them and understood the essence of what his father had signed. He was promised to wed Miss Jacinda Blanchett and they were to marry only if the lady so desired when she reached one-and-twenty. But no one knew where the child—Drew hesitated . . . no, she was a young lady by now—where the lady might be. It suddenly occurred to him that life on his own had been rather hurly-burly. What had it been like for a mere child with only a country maid to take care of her? Whatever would the girl be like after so many years out of society, in the company of heaven knows what kind of people. He couldn't bear thinking about it.

The captain read through the papers, then glanced up at Mr. Wormwood when the solicitor spoke. "Do you intend to go to Rowland Park, Captain Morrow? I'm certain your father would be most happy to see you."

Drew didn't know just yet what he would do. He'd expected to come and find out that his father was alive and well. He hadn't been prepared to hear that everything at home was worse than it had been when he'd fled eight years ago.

"I don't know, sir. I still have business here in London and my ship sails at the end of the month."

"Captain," the solicitor said, looking uncertain. "I know it's not my place to interfere, but you have a duty, if not to your father, then at least to your name. There is a cloud over the name of Morrow in your village. I don't expect you to care about a girl you scarcely knew, but at least your return home would go a long way to prove that neither you nor your father was involved in her father's death. Show the county you are willing to honor the agreement. I doubt it will be necessary; the girl isn't likely to turn up after all these years, no matter what the family solicitor claims."

The captain nodded, but strangely he found that he did care about what had become of the girl. Likely there was nothing he or his father could have done to pre-

vent what happened. If it turned out that the Morrows's
need for funds was at the root of what happened, Miss
Blanchett might have suffered for it for the last eight
years. He couldn't walk away with no regrets. "I think
I *shall* visit my father. Perhaps I should examine the
facts of Blanchett's death and see if there is anything I
can learn. Thank you, sir, and good evening."

Minutes later the captain stepped into the street and
looked in both directions, his mind too full of worries to
think clearly. It was only a little after six o'clock, but the
summer sun had sunk behind the buildings, leaving Ox-
ford Road in growing shadows. The people passing by
him on the streets hurried to get to the safety of their
homes before dark. Like most seaport towns, London was
a dangerous place after the sun went down, especially
near the poorer sections like the waterfront.

Drew pulled out his watch and realized he was late
to meet friends from Calcutta. They were probably already at the Three Cranes Tavern on the Thames. Un-
familiar with the large city, he hailed a hackney. His
mind filled with thoughts of his father, he took little
note of the grandeurs of London. He wasn't fool
enough to take all the blame on his shoulders for his
father's frailties, but Drew knew that he'd contributed
to the baron's suffering by not performing his famil-
ial duty. Life on his own had taught him that besides
friendship, the only sentiment that was real was the
bond between parent and child.

As expected, his business partners awaited him at
the inn. Captain Nate Robertson and Captain Harry
Lyons, like Drew, had gone to India with dreams of
riches. They'd met six years earlier in a waterfront
tavern in Calcutta and formed a lasting friendship.
The trio had found the path to what they sought by

sailing the dangerous China routes on leaky old frigates belonging to others. Unlike most of their compatriots, who'd arrived in India from the slums of London or by family tradition, these three young men were from well placed families. Each had his own reasons to take to the seas. Later, they'd pooled their funds and purchased a small ship, which Nate, the eldest and most experienced, had captained while Harry and Drew continued to work for others. Within a year, the *Lucky Dragon* had made three very successful trips to the China coast and two more ships, the *Flying Dragon* and the *Golden Dragon,* were added to the fleet and the China Dragon Trading Company was born. It had proven a major success.

Nate and Harry asked no questions as to why Drew was late. They knew he had personal business in London that involved his father. In time he would tell them about his meeting if there was something they needed to know. The trio of friends dined and discussed shipping business but Drew had difficulty concentrating on matters at hand. At nine o'clock, he called it a night. His friends encouraged him to summon a hackney, but Drew refused. He wanted to walk along the wharf back to the *Flying Dragon*, hoping the stroll would help him sort out his plans. He owed a responsibility to the Morrow name, but there was an equal debt to his friends and business partners. He couldn't simply walk away and leave them in the lurch.

The summer night was unusually warm. A low coal haze from cooking fires hung over the river, giving the dying twilight a purple hue. He strolled along, paying little heed to the women on the game who called to him to sample their well-exposed wares. Burly sailors hurried past him on their way home or to the local taverns after their long voyages.

His thoughts dwelled on what it would be like meeting his father again. Theirs had never been a close relationship, but Drew knew he was as much to blame for that as his father. He'd been rather wild back then, his father often gone to London. He'd given little thought to anything but what he wanted. Did his father blame him for all that had befallen Rowland Park since?

Still, had Drew stayed and married that sickly child, would it have made a difference? The image came to him of what it would be like had he not gone off to seek his fortune: he would be five-and-twenty, fully dependent on his father and about to wed Miss Blanchett. Very likely he would have become one of those reckless young men who littered the English countryside with little to fill their days but mischief. The very thought was untenable.

Drew stopped at a bend in the river where he could see the *Flying Dragon*'s stern in the distance. Lanterns had been lit by the night watch, the sails were furled, and the red flag with a black dragon swayed gently in the soft breeze at the rear. A sense of pride filled him. It hadn't merely been hard work that had gotten him his own ship, but determination and an innate ability to master the seas, as well as the good fortune to meet allies with a common goal. He was younger than most captains but his men trusted him and knew him to be fair and just.

In that instant he came to a decision. While he took care of matters at home, he'd have his first mate, Cedric Bradley, arrange a cargo for a local trip, perhaps to France or Dublin. That way—

Drew froze when a footfall sounded behind him. Before he could turn, his head exploded in a burst of pain and his world went black.

A ship's bell pierced the night air on the Deptford docks as two figures separated from the shadows and slipped along the newly built wharf. The pungent smell of briny muck and dead fish hung in the air, a sign that the tide was at low ebb. In the night sky a silver moon hung low above the horizon and glowed a bright orange through the evening haze. The intrepid pair paid no attention to the sights and smells that were so familiar.

Ben Trudeau, along with his friend, Gilbert Sprat, had business. They were in search of the masthead of the *White Heron*. It had sailed into harbor two weeks earlier but, like most inbound vessels, it was forced to sit at harbor waiting for a turn at the docks. London was one of the busiest ports in the world, especially now that the war with France had ended.

In the dark all the vessels looked alike to the two young men. "We ain't never goin' to find 'er in that forest of masts out there." Gilbert sniffled—a remnant of the cold that had laid him low for the last week. He leaned forward to peer at the name painted on the nearest ship, as if he could read. What he really looked for was a great white bird with wings that protruded from the carved masthead. This design was unique in a time when most merchant ships sported beautiful carved maidens at their bows.

While the boys stood at the water's edge, a door to the Flying Fish Tavern opened some twenty yards down the way, spilling yellow light onto the cobblestone street. Sev-

eral men stepped out into the night, their voices quarrel-
some, their words indistinct.

Ben grabbed his friend's shirt sleeve and pulled him
down behind some crates. "Hide, Gilby, it's the
Gangers."

Young Sprat didn't argue. He'd had a close call some
six months earlier with a Press Gang up near the Tower.
He'd heard the news that very afternoon that the
Gangers were working the docks to replenish the *HMS
Buckley's* crew, and the last thing the boy wanted was to
spend the next twenty years sailing with His Majesty's
fleet.

Gilbert rubbed his grimy sleeve under his nose as a
sneeze threatened. Ben's eyes widened in fear that they
would be discovered as the sound of footsteps grew
close. He covered his friend's mouth with his hand and
waited, hoping the Pressmen wouldn't hear. The fact
that the boys had no nautical skills didn't matter. The
captains of the fleet weren't so choosy when they found
a young lad they thought trainable.

Within minutes, the burly Gangers dragged a protest-
ing sailor past the crates. The captured seaman begged for
his freedom, but the men paid him no heed. One of the
Impressment men protested the poor pickings that
evening. "We needs to move back to the East India Docks
or the London Docks. Them tars ain't so slippery, Porter.
We done good up there."

Porter's voice echoed loudly over the open water.
"Aye, we'll go after we hand this one over to Wimberly,
if he ain't drunk a'ready."

The men had scarcely passed when Gilbert sneezed,
but fortunately it came out sounding like the squeak of a
mouse. The footsteps faded and the area fell silent.
Gilbert tugged at his friend's worn coat. "Let's go, Ben.

I'm thinkin' we ain't goin' to be doin' no mudlarkin' tonight."

At twelve, Ben was three years younger than his friend, but his sharp wit and ability to read had set him apart from the other lads in the rundown tenement house where he and Jacinda let rooms. He leaned around the crate and looked in both directions. "Ain't nothin' to fear. They're headin' back to the Rendezvous." He referred to the place where the Impressment Service ran their operation at St. Katherine's by the Tower.

Gilbert took no comfort that the men were returning to where they kept their victims until they were transported to the navy. "It's early, them bully lads might come back if they ain't got their lot."

"Don't worry so, Gil. There's plenty of places to hide. Besides, Timmons is expectin' us to be at the drop and he don't take kindly to lads what don't do as they ought. Don't dawdle. I want to be back home before Jack returns. You know I'm not to be out this late."

Ben pulled his friend up and they hurried along the wharf. A quarter mile further down they found the masthead they sought—the wooden bird in flight. Without a word, Ben tapped his friend and gestured at the *White Heron*, grinning. The two lads headed to the ladder, which led to the muddy banks exposed by low tide. Gilbert was on the first rung down when two men darted from the shadows.

"Run, Ben!" Gilbert shouted, then jumped backward into the black void. The last thing he saw as he plummeted was a large cudgel aimed at his friend's head. He landed in deep mud and rolled toward the water in an attempt not to bog down. He'd been a mudlark, as they dubbed the lads who waded into the Thames to catch illicit booty from their accomplices onboard the ships, since he was eleven. He'd learned the hard way how unforgiving the slimy sediment along the banks was on a body.

Muddy, Gilbert struggled to his feet. He dashed west along the riverbank, his feet slipping every few steps. He heard the sound of pursuing footsteps on the wharf above him. Fear only drove him to run harder.

Gilbert sprinted until he almost dropped. His lungs hurt so much he feared they would burst, and the urge to cough nearly overcame him. At last, he could go no further. Gasping, he pressed his thin body against the damp pylons that lined the wharf and listened. The only sound was the pounding of blood in his ears. He'd escaped but the Gangers had Ben.

A strangled cry surged from him. He'd heard the stories from old pressed sailors who'd survived their ordeal. They were only too willing to spin tales of the harsh life at sea: years of imprisonment on a ship, bad food, and the lash. Gilbert wouldn't let that happen to his friend. There was only one thing he could do. After a cautious look about, he slipped along in the shadows another twenty yards west before he recognized the Wapping New Stairs. In his fear he'd run directly toward the Rendezvous. His flight had also brought him closer to home. The stairs would return him to the docks. He climbed cautiously, listening for any sound that would alert him. He made it to the top unmolested, then looked left and right.

The River Thames Police office was on the corner, but all seemed to be quiet. He raced across the wharf and disappeared into a narrow alley that would take him to Ratcliffe Highway and to Jack.

* * *

Jacinda pulled the handle of the ink press across the paper, then lifted the handbill and looked at the image. The words announcing the hiring of a crew for the *India Princess* had printed without a smudge. "There's the last one, Mr. Skirven."

The printer peered over the top of his glasses from his desk at the rear of the dimly lit print shop. He was a thin man with hollowed cheeks and a fringe of brown hair just above his ears. The oil lamp on the desk cast a ghostly white glow to his face, making him look quite terrifying, but in truth he was a kind old man who'd given Jacinda a job with few questions about how a "lad" from the slums was so well read. "You're certain. Did you double check the count? I don't want the first mate of the *Princess* to come in here and try to wriggle out of payin'. A hundred exact."

"Exactly, sir. There's not a smudged page in the lot either." Jacinda's arms ached from pulling the press lever all day long, but she knew Mr. Skirven needed the business and she had stayed the two hours extra that it had taken.

The clock over the fire grate showed it was half past ten. She prayed that Ben hadn't been worried, or worse, gone out to roam the streets after finishing his work at Bixley's Warehouse, where he fed and watered the horses that pulled wagon loads of goods away from the wharves. Wapping was a major shipping area where the London Docks had been recently rebuilt, greatly increasing the number of ships. Sailors were a rough lot and were generally the only people on the streets after dark.

The old printer stood up, pushed the glassed up on his nose and smiled, "Then you best be headin' home, lad. It's late. I won't be needin' you for the next few weeks. I'm goin' to the country to visit my mother."

Jacinda's heart plummeted. Their funds were low. She would have to look for work elsewhere. She picked up the canvas bag she'd brought with her meal and hung the strap over her shoulder. She bid her employer goodnight, then stepped into the alley near Shadwell.

Despite her male attire, Jacinda knew that danger lurked on those dark streets. She hurried toward Ratcliffe Highway. The June heat had driven many residents out onto the streets that evening. Many of the shops had remained open late. Business had been good since the Treaty of Toulouse. Ships from the continent were again frequenting the harbor.

Tall for a female, Jacinda had no difficulty passing as a young man once she bound her bosom with muslin. She appeared to the world as a thin lad in her coarse spun green waistcoat, tan breeches, and nankeen jacket. Her sandy blond hair, cut short about her ears, was curly. She often kept it covered with a wide-brimmed hat that cast her face in shadows even on a sunny day. Tonight, she kept her head down to avoid eye contact with the sailors, watermen, and rat-catchers still going about their business in the streets. In truth, there was little about her to attract undue attention, but on the rough streets of Wapping, her slender frame would intimate no one.

Her willowy build was deceiving. Jacinda had grown strong with the various jobs she'd performed over the years. She'd insisted that she do her part to help earn money after the funds from her father's jewelry had been spent. It was strange, but in all the years she'd been in London, she'd never gone hungry or been without a roof over her head. Those few items Trudy had taken that night had gone a long way to keeping them fed the first few years. Johnny Trudeau had made up the difference when their money had run low. That is, when he had been in Town. Despite Trudy's objection, he'd continued to ride the Pike to supplement their income. Unfortunately he'd ridden off two years ago and never returned. It was a subject that she and Ben had avoided discussing, but Jacinda, deep in her heart, suspected that the highwayman had met with a musket ball on some lonely road in the north. It was doubtful they would ever know for sure.

In the eight long years since she'd left home, the only time Jacinda had ever considered returning to Chettwood was the winter Trudy had died of the ague. Only fifteen and uncertain about continuing to live apart from her family without Nurse, Jacinda had packed her bags and thought to go to her Uncle Matthew's house in Soho. But Johnny begged her to stay. By then, his wife had left him with their son, Ben, and he needed her to help him raise the boy. She'd agreed to stay, knowing that it still wasn't safe for her to return since her father's murderer had never been brought to justice.

She dutifully wrote a letter a year to her father's solicitor, but had never told him her whereabouts for fear that he would supercede her father's wishes and force her to return to Chettwood. Unfortunately, this secrecy meant he had no way to send her funds, even had he agreed to do so, which she doubted he would.

After Trudy's death, Johnny never cosseted Jacinda. For the first time she had had a chance to see something of how the lower classes live. Working odd jobs wasn't easy, but she much preferred the experience to the life she would have led had she remained in Millicent Markham's care. Her cousin had treated her like a fragile piece of china, and she had been cloistered in her room much of the time. Still, there was a part of her that was curious about those she'd left behind. What had it been like at the manor without her or her father? There was little doubt Millie would run things efficiently, thinking it her duty. At present Jacinda felt no real desire to go back, knowing someone there wished to do her harm. But one day she would return to be mistress of her own life and Chettwood Manor. For now, however, Ben needed her.

As she drew near the tenement house where she and Ben kept rooms, she could see the front door was open. Lili Le Beau, their neighbor, was seated on a small barrel on the stoop, fanning herself and talking with passersby, mostly the sailors. The buxom woman spotted Jacinda, and waved. "You're late, Jack, my boy."

A smile tipped Jacinda's mouth. Lili was a former actress without a company. The large woman well knew that "Jack" was, in fact, female. She had befriended Ben and Jacinda, taking them under her wing within a month of their arrival at the rooming house . . . and a rather large wing it was. Big boned and tall, Lili had a decided fondness for sweets and gin, a rather odd combination in Jacinda's opinion, but the only thing that would make the former thespian pass on a glass of spirits was marzipan, macaroons, or sticky buns. It was a weakness that had led to the ruination of her once neat figure. Despite that, she might have kept a position in one of the touring companies, but when she drank, she became a handful. Too often she got into fights with the other performers while in her cups. The sad truth was that she was as handy with her fives as some of the bear garden bruisers, and on a bad night she could leave many a black-eyed actor or actress in her wake. Her pugilistic prowess and not her ample proportions had ended her career of treading the boards.

At five-and-thirty, with her still-pretty face, she'd settled into a room off Brett Street in Wapping and did laundry and darning for sailors, shipbuilders, stevedores, and watermen. And when the occasional seafarer stayed overnight, none of the neighbors complained to the church warden, for Lili was as generous as she was large. Many a night she had a simple meal prepared when Jacinda came home late from one of her jobs, and Ben would be already fed and in bed.

Jacinda stopped to answer the woman's query about her late return. "There was extra work and I couldn't leave. Is Ben upstairs?" She put one foot on the stoop and waited while Lili called a greeting to the old watchman, George Olney, as he made his rounds and called the hour. Jacinda thought she detected the scent of gin on the wind and eyed Lili closely, but clearly the woman wasn't into her cups just yet, for there was no hint of the demon that would appear after a full bottle.

"Nay, the lad's off with Gilbert Sprat. I warned him how it would be when you got home and found him gone. But there's no talkin' to a cheeky pup like our Benny when he's wantin' to have a lark."

Jacinda didn't voice her concerns. It wasn't as if Lili could stop the lad when he wanted to have his way. Jacinda had begun to think that returning to Westbury would be the best thing for Ben, who was like a brother to her now. There she could see that he had proper schooling and provide a safe haven from the cutthroats and ne'er-do-wells of this world. Who would have thought they would not have found her father's killer by now? She bid Lili goodnight, then climbed the stairs to the small room where she and Ben lived.

Warm, stale air greeted her. She lit the rush lamp on the rickety table covered with a faded blue gingham cloth. The light illuminated their few belongings: sleeping pallets they'd purchased cheaply at one of the local stores where the sailors shopped, an ancient cabinet filled with their bits of crockery, and a tattered old painted screen behind which Jacinda dressed.

She pulled one of the table's three chairs to the window, which looked out over Ratcliffe Highway. She lifted the latch and pushed opened the shutter, releasing the heat before she settled into the chair to await Ben's return. The long cobblestone road below disappeared into the darkness. She watched the throng of sailors, both foreign and English, come and go from the taverns, which wouldn't close until midnight. A slight breeze came out of the west. With it came the smell of tar and newly milled timber from the nearby shipyards, but at least it helped to cool the room.

What could Ben be doing so late? She worried about him because he, like many of the Wapping lads, always had some get-rich-quick scheme in the works. He knew the truth about her legacy, but to him it was only a story. Over the years it seemed that he had come to doubt she was in danger and that she would one day be wealthy. Her lips curled upward when she thought about what Ben's reaction would be when he saw Chettwood for the first time.

Then the smile disappeared. *If* she ever returned home again. The thought of going back to Cousin Millie's iron rule was not the least bit enticing. Jacinda lived her life much as she wanted, and she wasn't certain she wished the rigid structure of a young lady's world again, to be idle and bored out of her wits day in and day out.

The thumping of footsteps on the stairs made her turn around with anticipation. But to her dismay the door burst open and only Gilbert Sprat entered. His hat was missing, his face was flushed beneath muddy streaks. It was an obvious sign he'd been down at the docks, where she'd expressly forbidden Ben to go. The lad could barely catch his breath as he coughed. "They've . . . taken 'im."

Jacinda rose even as her heart sank. There could be no doubt about the " 'im" to whom the boy referred. "Who has taken him?"

"The Impress is out. Tryin' to refill the ships what took such a thrashin' from the Yanks." Even a lad like Gilbert was aware of the American victories in the recent naval war. "They took 'im to St. Katherine's Rendezvous."

Jacinda's knees grew weak and she sank back into the chair. What could she do? She hadn't the money to bribe the Gangers to release the boy. And once they put the men on the barge it was almost impossible for them to get free unless the navy deemed them unseaworthy, which wasn't likely to happen to a healthy lad like Ben. A sob escaped Jacinda and she put her head down in her hands. She couldn't think of Ben forever lost to her.

"Lud, child, yer filthy," Lili called from the doorway. "Ye dashed past like a banshee was after ye. Where's Ben?"

"He's been pressed, Miss Lili," Gilbert cried.

Jacinda lifted her head, tears still streaming down her face. "What can we do, Lil?"

"Hush now, child, and let me think." After several minutes of stomping round the room softly swearing, she stopped. A martial light came into the large woman's eyes. "I'll tell ye what we're goin' to do. Ye dry yer eyes and listen to me, Jack." With that, the woman laid out the plan. Jacinda and Gilbert listened and nodded.

For the first time since the boy had brought the news

about Ben, Jacinda had hope. She put her hand on Lili's arm. "Do you think it will work?"

A twinkle glinted in Lili's gray eyes. "It did in Bristol about ten years ago. I read about it in the local papers when I was out touring with my last company of players. Two lasses pulled it off and so can we. Give me five minutes to get ready and we're for St. Katherine's. You"—she grabbed Gilbert's collar and shoved him into the hall—"go home, wash, and stay there. If this goes awry, we don't want you caught."

He looked from Lili to Jacinda, about to protest.

"Go, Gilbert." Jacinda ordered. "If we're caught there's little they can do but turn us over to the magistrate, but you would likely end up in the navy."

An uncertain look came into the lad's eyes. "Aye." He started down the stairs then stopped and looked back at the two women. "Bring Ben home, please."

"We'll do our best, lad," Lili called as she swept across the hall to her room.

Jacinda went to the small hearth and found the tool she would need, then went out to await her friend. The door to Lili's room stood ajar. In a matter of minutes the actress reappeared at her table. Her golden blonde curls had been combed away from her face, which gave her a much younger appearance. The rouge on her lips and cheeks made her prettier than Jacinda had ever seen. A strong scent of floral perfume wafted on the air and the tucker had been removed from the blue stripped gown Lili wore, exposing a great deal of her ample charms to the world. A pretty lace shawl was draped low over her shoulders. From the table, she picked up a half bottle of gin. She held it up and took one last swig and sighed. Then she took a brown flask and poured a small amount of liquid into the gin. She replaced the stopper and shook the bottle. With one last regretful look at the bottle, she thrust it into her tatted reticule and stepped into the hall.

"Come, Jack, you must do exactly what I tell you. Do you have what you need?"

Jacinda pulled the tool from under her coat.

Lili nodded. "Very well, we are off."

They made their way to the street where traffic had grown light. Jacinda offered Lili an arm as if she were a true gentlemen and they set off for St. Katherine's Rendezvous.

Don't worry, Ben, Jacinda whispered to herself, *we're coming to rescue you.*

CHAPTER TWO

Drew's head throbbed as consciousness drifted just beyond his grasp. A wave of nausea curled in his stomach and he feared he might be sick. If only he could open his eyes. Jumbled images flashed though his brain, leaving him disoriented. Was he still battling a bout of fever in Calcutta? He remembered the tender mercies of the old Chinese herbalist his friends had found to treat him. The illness had been years ago. The image disappeared and another took shape. Drifting on a sea of darkness . . . visions from Madras surface. A knife wound from one of the drunken sailors on shore. But he dismissed the memory since this pain was in his head.

With a determined struggle, Drew opened his eyes but saw only darkness surrounding him. He blinked twice to make certain his eyes were truly open. A soft groan sounded nearby and he knew he was awake. He took no comfort from that fact that he wasn't alone in his torment. As he tried to move toward the sound, another wave of pain surged through his head. He leaned back against the wall and tried to think, tried to recall where he was and what he was doing in this dark place with others who seemed to be suffering as much as he. Everything was mixed up in his head. He'd departed India months earlier. Had his ship been taken over by pirates? No, the *Flying Dragon* was harbored in London. He remembered the crew had been paid off and his first mate was seeing to stores and cargo for another trip.

A heavy weight formed in his chest when the day's events came flooding into his foggy brain. The visit to his father's solicitor—Blanchett dead, the daughter missing, the decision he'd made to do something about it. He'd had dinner with his friends to tell them he wasn't returning to Calcutta immediately . . . or did he tell them of the decision? He pressed his eyes closed as the pain in his head throbbed with the beat of his heart. When he lifted a hand to his temple, the clank of a chain sounded and a heavy iron cuff slid down his wrist. He extended his arm and realized he was chained to the wall. His thoughts scattered a bit and he couldn't think why he would be in prison.

Another groan sounded further away in the darkness and a young voice cried, "Oh, Jack, I'm sorry," then diminished into a whimper.

Drew gathered his wits and took stock. The musty smell of wet wood, unwashed bodies, and stale gin surrounded him in the darkness. As he strained to listen, he could hear water lapping on the wooden wall behind him. Was he in the hole of a ship? If so, they hadn't yet set sail, for there were no swells or waves rocking them.

The soft crying continued and despite his own dire circumstances, Drew took pity on what was clearly a young boy. "What's your name, lad?"

After a loud sniffle, a timorous voice answered, "Ben, sir, Ben Trudeau."

Drew could hear fear in the boy's voice and thought to keep him talking. "Do you know where we are, Ben?"

"Aye, we're in a barge what the Gangers use to transport men to the fleet, sir."

Drew's stomach plummeted. Great heavens, he'd managed to get himself pressed. A vague memory of being on the East India Docks flashed in his mind but he couldn't bring the actual event into focus. As a seasoned sailor and ship's officer, he would be considered valuable to the Impressment Service and that would make it all the more difficult to escape his fate. At present his head hurt too much for him to even try to reason out what he could do. Perhaps there was nothing to do but pray. He'd been around docks in enough seaports to know that His Majesty's officers showed little concern for those who'd been caught in their sweep for new recruits. They needed men and that was that.

Drew leaned his head back and tried to concentrate on something other than the pain and the sick feeling in the pit of his stomach. But the word "pressed" and all that it meant continued its endless swirl in his brain.

The street lamp's dim yellow glow brightened a narrow stretch of street near the Tower of London. A forest of ships' masts cluttered the night sky ahead of them as Jacinda and Lili made their way through the dark alley to the Impressment Service's Rendezvous beside the River Thames. From Thames Street they heard a watchman call the hour as midnight and they paused to listen, but only the sounds of the river greeted them. At this late hour, few lights twinkled at them from Southwark on the far side of the river. The stench of fish, rotting food, and bilge in the water almost overpowered Jacinda. A longing to see the lovely River Axe, so near to Chettwood Manor, filled her.

Lili squeezed Jacinda's hand, then put a finger over her lips and pointed to the lone guard, who lounged on a stack of old fishing nets stacked on crates at the wharf's edge. The roof of the Impressment barge was just visible in the water below him. A small lantern on deck hung on a peg and illuminated a closed door at the entrance to the cabin below.

Jacinda's pulse jumped at the thought of Ben being alone in that dank, dark place. She resisted the impulse to rush the man on the wharf, knowing that such a noise would likely bring others from the Press Gang to his aid. If she got Ben safely back, she would need to find a way to take him to Chettwood. She was no longer a child and could take care of herself, and Ben was getting to an age where he was vulnerable to the dangers of a big city. But first she had to get Ben off that barge. She prayed that whatever Lili had poured into the gin would work quickly.

The large woman stepped into her role with ease. She patted her hair, then strolled across the damp cobblestones, humming a cheerful ditty, until she reached the wharf. She pretended to spy suddenly the guard, whose wary attention had locked on her the moment she stepped into the glow of the lamplight. The man appeared to be in his thirties and was dressed in the Impressment uniform of ivory canvas breeches, stripped shirt, and blue coat. His round black hat sat low over a bush of dark hair.

The sound of Lili's voice barely reached Jacinda in her hiding place.

"Well, and here I was thinkin' I'd have to drink alone this starry night." Lili pulled the stopper from the bottle. She pressed the stem to her lips as if she were taking a large swallow. She wiped her mouth, then said, "Oh, and ye be a handsome fellow at that."

The ganger licked his lips and grinned, his gaze moving from the bottle to her ample bosom, then back to the bottle. "Yer a fine lookin' lass. I'd be 'appy to share your refreshment."

Lili giggled, then made her way over to where he waited. At the last moment, she pretended to lose her balance and tumbled into the man's lap. There was a great deal of laughter and Jacinda couldn't make out what the man whispered to Lili and she wasn't certain she wanted to know.

Lili handed him the bottle and whispered into his ear. He took a good swig, gave a hearty laugh, and nuzzled her neck. Jacinda's cheeks warmed as she watched the man's hand wander over the larger woman's curves. She knew she would owe their neighbor a large debt for what she was enduring for them. Lili playfully batted his hand away and said, "Why, yer a naughty one. Lucky me." He chuckled and again drank from the bottle.

The next fifteen minutes seemed an eternity to Jacinda as she sat crouched behind the boxes, half afraid to watch what was happening on the crate. But Lili was masterful and it took only a short time for the man to finish the gin. Jacinda's knees grew stiff and her patience short, but she stayed where she was until the ganger's head slumped against Lili's shoulder. The woman lifted his head and called to him. When she received no response, she slid to her feet. She signaled to Jacinda.

After a quick glance about revealed no one nearby, Jacinda dashed across the road to the wharf while Lili pushed the unconscious man over onto the fishing net, making sure he wouldn't fall off.

The Tower Stairs led to the water and took Jacinda to the muddy river bank. She scrambled over the gangway onto the gently rocking barge. Moments later Lili stood behind her, lamenting the ruination of her best slippers by the mud.

Mentally Jacinda promised to buy her friend ten pairs if they all got out of this unscathed. She scanned the wharf for movement but all was quiet. Uncertain what they would find inside, Jacinda slowly pulled open the door to the lower cabin. Darkness loomed, so she lifted the lantern from the peg and went down the steps.

To her horror, she discovered ten males, mostly young men shackled to the walls. Some were asleep; others shielded their eyes from the glare of the lantern. Her instinct was to find Ben first, but how could she ignore these lads, each and every one of whom had family who likely didn't know where they were at that moment.

Lili stepped into the small space behind her. "The Gangers have been busy I see. You start on the left, Jack, I'll work on the right. The large woman pulled a hammer from beneath her skirts and smashed the wall of the barge where the first chain connected to the wall. "We're here to set you free, lads."

There was a stirring among the captives, but they fell silent as Lili give the bolt two more good whacks with her hammer and it broke free. Jacinda, released from her dilemma of where to start, pulled the small ax from her coat and began work on the opposite wall. When the first man was free, she said, "Go up and keep watch."

"Aye, lad, and may God bless ye." He rose and moved past her as she began on the next set of chains bolted to the wall. She'd released three lads when Ben tugged on her leg. "I knew you'd come, Jack." She hugged him, then with two forceful strokes of the ax had him free. "Get up on deck, if you see someone coming, shout a warning, then run."

"I won't leave without you and Lil."

"Don't be a fool. You know we're in no danger." She gave him a knowing look and the boy's eyes widened in understanding. He gave her a hug, then raced up the stairs. Jacinda moved further down to the last man and noted that of the captives, he alone was dressed as a gentleman. His head was leaned again the wall and blood oozed from a wound at his temple. A cockade hat lay beside him on the floor, yet he wore no uniform. A merchant sailor perhaps? If so he would be very valuable to the navy, who were always looking for experienced men. She looked around and realized that Lil had finished and gone topside; only she and the gentleman remained.

She asked, "Are you able to run, sir?"

He groaned, and lifted his head. "I'll make it lad, if you'll finish the job of freeing me." He tugged on the chains that still held him to the wall.

A strange sensation raced through her. It was almost as if she knew him . . . but how could that be? Thinking it was just her heightened nerves betraying her, she gave the bolt two quick strikes and the man gave it a mighty tug. It pulled free, and he tried to struggle to his feet. Jacinda hesitated a moment as her old fear of strangers surfaced. It had haunted her since the night in the rocks. She pushed the anxiety aside, knowing this man needed her assistance. She took his arm and helped him rise. He swayed as he stood and put a hand to his head.

"Sorry, I'm not as steady on my feet as I thought. Lead the way."

Jacinda watched him swaying and without a word, pulled his arm over her shoulder. "Lean on me, sir." They made their way up the stairs on the deck. Strangely, she was very conscious of the feel of his well-muscled build through his coat when he leaned against her. This was no Town Tulip, but a man of activity. She pushed the thoughts aside and concentrated on leading him out of danger.

He swore softly as the gentle rocking of the barge forced him to lean into her support. Intuitively she sensed that he hated that the injury had made him momentarily defenseless. The smell of tobacco and some exotic spice pleasantly teased her nose. She'd never met a man whose scent was so enticing. It tickled at some old memory, but she didn't have the time to put her mind to the matter.

After some careful maneuvering of the steps, they stood on deck and the cool evening air was a welcome change from the barge's stifling heat. Jacinda stepped away from the gentleman, who seemed to be finding his legs. He ran a hand through his hair and then tested the lump at his scalp, winching when his fingers pressed too hard.

Jacinda's gaze roved over the waterfront. All the freed men had disappeared into the night. Only Lili and Ben stood watch on the wharf, looking east toward the London Docks. Lili gestured for Jacinda and the gentleman to join them on dry land. "Jack, I can hear the Gangers comin' back with more captured sailors. Best get Ben and your new friend out of here."

"What about you, Lili?" Jacinda urged the injured gentleman towards the gangway, following close behind, ready to lend a hand should he need her.

"Don't worry about me. I can make my way home alone."

On the wharf, Ben had taken an interest in the unconscious guard. "Is he dead?"

"Don't be silly," Lili said. "He's drugged." She turned to Jacinda. "I'll see you back at the rooms. Go, child. I'm in no danger . . . just a female out for a walk. I don't know anythin' about escaped seamen."

Once safely on the wharf, Jacinda eyed the gentleman in the dim light from the street lamp. Again the strange feeling of familiarity came over her. Did she know him? She dismissed the thought as foolish. She could scarcely see him in this light. Besides, she knew no gentlemen in London, especially not one so tall and athletic in build. "Can you walk without assistance, sir?"

He ran a hand over his waistcoat, tugging the bottom as he swayed slightly, then he gave a shaky laugh. "I'll make myself to get away from here. I owe you a debt I can never repay. What's your name, my boy?"

"Jack, Jack Trudeau." She used the name she'd adopted since donning men's clothing. "You'd best go home, sir. The Gangers are coming back." In the distance she could hear the approaching Impressment men and their complaining prisoners. Clearly they were too engaged in their task to take notice of those under the street lamp.

"The problem is," the man said, still seemingly a bit dazed as he looked about in puzzlement, "I have no home at present save my ship and I don't know London; I'm captain of the *Flying Dragon* out of Calcutta. She's at the East India Docks. I'm Captain—"

A shout rang out down the wharf. They'd been spotted by the returning Press Gang. Sounds of rapidly approaching footsteps echoed over the water.

Ben dashed into the shadows of the Tower and Jacinda followed, calling over her shoulder. "Follow us, sir. We'll lead you safely back to the docks you want."

The injured gentleman didn't need any urging. He loped after the disappearing pair into the dark alley. His steps were a bit uneven, but he trailed his rescuers since his life depended on evading the pursuers.

Ben led the way, having more experience than Jacinda in this part of London. They headed due north, away from the river, with the shouts of the Impressment men ringing in their ears. They kept to the byways and alleys, running at a steady pace. At this late hour the only sound was the pounding of their feet on the cobblestones. The gentleman's ability to keep up was limited and Jacinda was forced several times to go back and beckon him around a corner, calling, "This way, Captain," for that was all she knew of him.

By the time they'd traversed almost four long blocks, they were winded. Ben led them into a small alleyway where they could rest and catch their breath as well as take stock of their situation. The trio could do little but gasp for breath. At last, Ben edged back to the opening at Smithfield Street to look for their pursuers. Before he even reached the main street, the sound of racing footsteps approached. Ben backed away and ducked behind a crate even as Jacinda and the captain moved deeper into the alley. The pressmen raced past.

Jacinda held her breath and prayed the men wouldn't realize they'd lost their quarry in the dark. But by the time the pursuers reached the corner, it was evident they would go no further. The men milled about while they discussed what was to be done. Jacinda and the others were trapped where they were, for the alley was a dead end.

Within minutes, the Press Gang began to work their way back towards where the three were hidden, searching the alcoves and alleys. Ben moved deeper into the dead end lane and whispered, "They're comin' back."

The captain softly called to Ben and Jacinda, "This way." He gestured to a set of wooden stairs that gleamed brightly in the moonlight. The stairway tiers went up several stories on the side of the warehouse. At first Ben shook his head and Jacinda could only stare in horror. Perhaps the only thing that frightened her more than strangers was heights, a fact that Ben well knew.

He moved back to the mouth of the alley but when the searchers drew near, he returned to where Jacinda was crouched. "We'd best go up or they'll find us." He squeezed her hand and she knew she had to go for his sake.

"Come, lads," the captain called in a whisper from the first landing. "There's no time to delay."

He led the way, moving lightly on the wooden steps. Ben stopped to test each door on their upward climb, but all were locked. As she climbed higher, Jacinda had a bad feeling that all their efforts that night had been for naught. The Press Gang would get Ben after all. A sick feeling filled her stomach but whether more from frustration or fear, she was uncertain. All she knew was not to look down.

At the top landing, which ended at a locked door, the captain awaited them. He pointed across the railing. "Do you lads think you can make the jump?" The flat roof of the warehouse next door spread out in front of them like a welcoming field. Moonlight glinted off the slate tiles and chimney pots, dimly illuminating the way to safety. Unfortunately, the gap between the stairway and the roof was a gaping four-foot-wide crevasse.

Ben looked at Jacinda, who did her best to keep the fear from her voice. "Go. Don't worry about me." He hesitated a moment, then saw something in her face that reassured him. He didn't say a word; he merely climbed over the rail and with a leap cleared the open space that separated the building and the stairs.

"You next, Jack," the captain urged.

Knees shaking, Jacinda climbed over the rail. She tried not to look down but she couldn't bring herself to jump.

"Go, lad, go!"

"I-I cannot, I—" but before Jacinda could finish, the captain climbed over the rail and pried her hand free.

"Come! And here we go!"

She had no time to protest; she was forced into the air, the man holding her wrist tightly even as her stomach seemed to be in her throat. They hit the roof hard but the captain helped her keep her footing. Jacinda's spirits soared. They were once again on the move.

Behind them shouts sounded from the alley below. Her elation evaporated—they'd been seen.

The captain, still holding her arm, pulled her across the roof to the opposite side where Ben stood peering over the ledge. "There's no stairway, we're trapped."

Behind them, a shouted, "Halt in His Majesty's name!"

A quick glimpse over the edge was all Jacinda allowed herself before she moved back from the edge, but that was enough. Her throat tightened and tears pricked at her eyes. Their options had run out. "I'm sorry, Ben."

To Drew Morrow, the lad's voice sounded utterly devastated and as soft as a girl's. He stared hard at the boy, but in the darkness he could see little because a long-brimmed hat shadowed the lad's face. Drew thought it was just a trick of sound that had made the boy's voice

sound so feminine. He owed Jack Trudeau and his
brother a great deal at the moment. It was a debt that he
fully intended to repay. But they hadn't escaped yet.

Drew was no fool about their chances if they were re-
captured. He suspected that if enough money could
change hands with the Press Men, he might be able to
buy his way free, but he doubted he could do the same
for two such healthy lads from the tenements. Unfortunately, at the moment, he had scarcely two pounds on
him, having taken his first mate's advice about not carrying large sums in London. Truth be told, he couldn't
be sure what sum was sufficient for a bribe if the Navy's
need was great.

Determined to find a solution to their dilemma, his
gaze searched the street below for an escape. They had
to get off that roof if they were to have a chance. As
footsteps hammered on the wooden stairway in the
alley, Drew spotted their salvation. "There," he called,
drawing the lads' attention to a wagon which rolled up
the street in their direction. It was a huge rag wagon on
its journey to the paper factory. "We can jump and the
rags will break our fall."

"Jump!" the older Trudeau cried. "Have you taken
leave of your senses, sir? Why, it's over two stories
down. If we miss we'll break both legs or worse, be
killed."

Drew looked over his shoulder and saw that the Press
Gang had reached the top of the stairs. "We go now,
Jack, or all is lost."

Plucky to the core, Ben shrugged. "I'm jumpin', Jack.
Besides, if I miss the wagon, them fellows can't take me
with a broken peg." The lad climbed on the ledge and
leapt into thin air as the wagon pulled beneath them.
Drew and Jacinda leaned over and prayed the boy

wouldn't miss. Ben landed in the pile of rags with a bounce and without a sound. He stood and urgently gestured for them to follow.

Remembering his rescuer's earlier fright, Drew grabbed Jack's hand and pulled the lad onto the ledge when he climbed up. "We must go now or miss our chance." Her hand twitched in his.

"No, I cannot. You go. I'll be fine." Jack tried to pull away but Drew slid an arm around him, refusing to let go.

It struck Drew that Jack was rather delicate despite the courage he'd shown that evening. "We'll go together, lad. Close your eyes."

Drew could hear loud thumps of the Press Gang as they landed on the roof behind them. He pushed Jack along the ledge to compensate for the slow-moving wagon, then judged the right angle to jump so as not to land on Ben. With a whispered prayer, he tightened his hold on the lad and leapt out over the wagon. The ground rushed up at them and thankfully the wagon was beneath them when they landed.

Drew, positioned at the rear and unable to move or risk missing the wagon altogether, caught his right foot on the edge of the wagon's wooden side. It twisted to the left and pain shot up his leg.

He had no time to worry about his injury. He rolled away from Jack, who lay with his eyes closed, still trembling. "Ben, tell the driver there are two pounds in it for him if he can keep us from the clutches of the Press Gang."

The captain couldn't hear the lad and the driver's conversation, but suddenly the wagon jolted and swayed as it picked up speed, taking them away from the men up on the roof, who shouted at them in frustration. The wagon rounded the corner onto Smithfield Street which would take them east towards Wapping.

No traffic obstructed the rough trip up Smithfield which soon turned into Ratcliffe Highway. The old rag wagon was not designed for such treatment as the driver was currently inflicting, but despite its rattling and swaying, it kept moving away from danger. Jacinda lay in the smelly rags, ashamed of her conduct on the roof. If it hadn't been for the captain she would have been too afraid to jump. She was thankful he had been there and for the ragman's timely appearance below them. Still, she was anxious to return to the protection of their rooms. She wouldn't feel completely safe until then and she was worried about Lili. Would their friend, who'd done so much, make it safely back home?

Gathering her dignity, she sat up and recognized the shops they passed. They were almost at the street where she and Ben lived. A backward glance to make certain they weren't being pursued and she noticed the captain rubbing his ankle. "Are you hurt, sir?"

"Nothing of consequence, lad. In truth, my head hurts worse than my ankle."

In the glow from an oil street lamp on the corner, Jacinda could see him in profile as he smiled and took note of how few lines etched his smooth face. Curiously, he seemed far too young to be the captain of a ship. Her years spent in Wapping and Shaddock had caused her to rub elbows, so to speak, with a variety of sailors from ships' cooks to officers. Captains were generally weather-worn gentlemen even when they weren't very old. It was clear he hadn't been sailing for many years.

Ben scrambled to the back of the wagon, interrupting

Jacinda's contemplation of their companion. "I've talked the driver into stopping at New Gravel Lane to let us down. We'll be close to home there and the East India docks are just a short walk."

The captain reached into his coat and handed Ben the coins. "Give him my thanks."

Some five minutes later, the wagon drew to a halt. The trio climbed down and the rag wagon continued on at a more sedate pace. Ratcliffe Highway was quiet; only the occasional drunken sailor could be heard singing an off-key sea verse in the distance as he made his way back to his rooms for the night.

The captain's ankle was clearly bothersome, so Ben and Jacinda helped him back to their tenement with the offer of a ride from one of their neighbors who operated a hackney. The stairway to their lodgings was too narrow for three across so Jacinda hurried ahead. She stopped first to knock at Lili's door, but as she expected, Lili was not yet returned. While unlocking their door, she was suddenly aware of the musty odor of humanity that filled the halls and she wished they had someplace better to bring a gentleman, but this was all they could afford. She relit the old rush lamp as well as two tallow candles she'd purchased the week before. She looked around and determined that while the room was sparsely furnished, it was clean. They had nothing to feel ashamed about here. She set about finding something for them to slake their thirst and found a jug of apple cider that she'd bought at the Pear Tree on her way home the night before.

Minutes later, Ben helped the captain through the door. The gentleman settled in one of the ladder-back chairs and Ben lifted his injured leg to an opposite one. Busy putting cups on the table for all three, a gasp escaped Jacinda's lips when the gentleman looked up at her and smiled. "Lads, I owe you a great deal."

The light from the lamp glimmered on his face. It was her first clear look at the man. He was as handsome as she had suspected, but that wasn't what had caught her attention. A tiny half moon scar that arched downward from his eye seemed to leap out at her. Could it be? On closer inspection, it was a more mature face than she remembered with its now angular planes, but she would have known him anywhere had she encountered him in the light of day.

Andrew Morrow! One of the very people she suspected had been involved with her father's murder. She took a step back, stunned to be face-to-face with a man she'd reviled in her mind so many times.

His gaze searched her face for a moment and a tiny crease appeared at his brow. "Are you well, Jack? You look as if you'd seen a ghost." His frown increased as his gaze played over her features. "Have we met before, lad? On the wharf when my ship ported or some other place?"

Jacinda turned away as she pulled the stopper from the cider, suddenly afraid he might recognize her. "I think not, sir, unless you have spent time here in the Wapping printshop where I was employed." She poured out the cider with shaking hands as she asked over her shoulder, "You never finished telling us who you are, sir."

"Aye, we were interrupted, were we not? I'm Captain Drew Morrow of the *Flying Dragon* out of Calcutta, formerly of Somerset. May I say I'm quite happy to have made your acquaintance."

A wave of dizziness that rivalled what she'd experienced on the warehouse roof overcame her. She'd envisioned her meeting with him many times over the years and in her imagination she'd rained accusations over his head. But somehow, the callow youth in her imagination was nothing like the self-assured Captain Morrow seated at her table. The sulky lad had been replaced by a kind, confident gentleman. But then, she most certainly wasn't that fragile little girl who'd met him in her father's great hall, so why should she have expected him to have remained the same?

A sharp pain pierced her thoughts and her anger was renewed as memories from the night her father died resurfaced. Had this man been involved? He had been scarcely more than a lad at the time and he'd seemed more intent on getting away from them than on wanting to hurt them. Besides, she couldn't forget that he'd saved her on the roof tonight. He could have left her behind on two occasions but had chosen to help her jump instead. Was such a man capable of murder? Her mind was in chaos as she moved around the table, not listening to Ben's chatter.

The gentleman took the cup and drank thirstily. The drink and Ben's gabbling soon distracted him from inspecting her, and she moved away from the light at the table after pouring a cup of cider for Ben. The boy was answering the captain's questions about their life in Wapping and Morrow was surveying their tiny room. Ben dutifully told the tale that most of the neighbors had heard. *Two brothers from Bristol come to London to eke out a living now that their mother was gone and their father's fate unknown.* When pressed as to where their father had gone, Ben grew vague, saying, "up north to work," then changed the subject.

"Bristol! I'm going home to Rowland Park, which is quite near there." Drew's face took on a faraway look as he stared at the flame flickering in the lamp. "I've much to make up for in my past."

With her back to the man she should hate, Jacinda sensed pain and remorse in those words. "You did something you regret?" Had he destroyed Lord Rowland's dreams of money by the act of killing her father? Trembles at the recollection of that horrid night seemed to rove all over her body. She peeked over her shoulder, trying to imagine him involved in such dark doings. There was something in his well-featured face that had almost convinced her she was wrong, when Trudy's final words rang in her head.

"Trust no one, child. Someone you least suspect might wish you harm. Promise me you will trust no one until the truth is revealed." Jacinda stiffened her spine. She mustn't let down her guard with Andrew Morrow or anyone else until the murder was solved.

The gentleman's reply interrupted her thoughts. "Yes, but then I would guess most young men disappoint their fathers at some point in time." The captain stared into his cup a moment in a brown study, then seemed to shake off his melancholy. "I made a dreadful mistake and I'm hoping he will forgive me. But you can have little interest in my problems." He stood. "I must be going. Is there anything I can do for you lads to repay my debt?"

He was about to leave Jacinda with even more questions than when he'd come. A strong need to know what mistake he'd made filled Jacinda. How could she allow him to walk away from them without knowing, without asking . . . but that would reveal her true identity. She needed more time. A sudden inspiration filled her. The only way to find out the truth was to go back and face her enemy, whoever that might be. She'd decided to return to Chettwood earlier that evening, but here was an opportunity that was even better: to return to the county in her new guise.

"I need employment, sir, and we were thinking of returning home." She saw the surprise in Ben's face but he kept silent as she continued. "If you are going to Somerset, would you take us with you?"

The gentleman eyed the two lads a moment, then smiled. "Do either of you know anything about horses or farming?"

Ben jumped to his feet. "I do, sir. The Smithy just beyond the Pear Tree pays me to groom the prads stabled there that are used at the warehouses."

"What about you, Jack? What skills do you possess?" Captain Morrow quirked a brow at Jacinda.

"I can read, sir. " Seeing the surprise in his eyes, she added, "My mother was a nursery maid and learned the words with her charges." Since coming to London she'd used that explanation often to explain her ability in this world of poverty and illiteracy, often praying that her lady mother would forgive her for such a fabrication.

The gentleman nodded. "Then I'm certain we can find something for you to do at my father's estate. If nothing else I'll hire you on to the *Flying Dragon* once I move it to Bristol." He looked uncertain for a moment, and Jacinda suspected he didn't know what kind of welcome he would receive on his own, much less bringing servants along. But the uncertainty disappeared from his eyes and he ruffled Ben's hair. "I shall be here at ten o'clock sharp in the morning. Be ready to go." He tested his ankle. It seemed improved. Ben hurried to the first floor to wake Harry Nicks, who owned the hackney.

Some ten minutes later, a sleepy Harry arrived in front of the tenement house with his cab and the captain again thanked Jacinda and Ben for saving him. He climbed in and said good-bye. As the hackney disappeared into the night, Ben turned to Jacinda, placing his arms akimbo. "Why are we going to Somerset? If it's about my gettin' caught by the Pressmen, I swear I won't go—"

Jacinda put her hand on his shoulder, to stop a promise that he would never be able to keep. "It's time I began the search for my father's murderer, and it just so happens Chettwood is next door to the captain's home."

Before Ben could comment, a very tired Lili came out of the darkness on Ratcliffe Road. Jacinda hugged the large woman and urged her to their room for something to drink. It was only after Ben had finally crawled into bed that Jacinda informed their friend of the plan to return to Somerset.

"So you've decided to go home at last." There was sadness in Lili's voice. "It's a good thing, child, even though I shall miss ye. Ye've no business here in the slums of London."

Jacinda put a hand over her friend's. "I'll send for you as soon as I'm able."

"Nonsense, child, I've no more business living in the wilds of Somerset than ye have in this squalor of Wapping."

"But I want to do something to help you as you have helped Ben and me."

Lili grinned "I did very little . . . but I wouldn't take exception to a bit of help with opening a little sewing shop in say, Deptford or Shadwell." Her eyes twinkled at the idea of having her own place.

"I promise, as soon as I may, I shall buy you a place

but it cannot be until I come of age." A strained look passed over Jacinda's face. "If I manage to survive until then."

Lili hugged Jacinda. "I'm certain ye can do anything ye set your mind to child. Look what ye've done raising Ben alone in one of the roughest parts of London. Besides, ye'll have an advantage of that disguise and our Ben to watch out for ye. He can be quite fierce when needs be." Lili walked to the door, about to depart. "I'll see ye off in the morning and remember, if ye need me, I'll come at once." With that she said good night and left Jacinda.

She walked to the window and looked out. Lil was right. She could do this. Still, an uncomfortable fear swirled in her stomach as she thought about facing Andrew Morrow in the morning. What if he remembered who she was? Then she reminded herself that he'd met her only once, in the great hall at Chettwood. There was little likelihood of him connecting a scrawny girl from Westbury with a grown lad from London. Feeling more confident about what she intended to do, she went to bed.

CHAPTER THREE

Two days later on a warm June afternoon, Drew tooled his newly procured curricle and four along the road from Wells. Given the little amount of time he'd had, the vehicle was superbly sprung and the cattle excellent goers. The journey from London had been easy and the weather fine.

The Mendip Hills loomed to the north, the Somerset Levels spread out to the south, their fields abundant with the coming harvest. Since entering Somerset, they'd passed numerous orchards with trees heavy with apples to make the cider for which the county was famous. The thought of a tankard of cider and a wedge of cheese from Cheddar Gorge made Drew's mouth water. He'd spent many a summer afternoon on these very roads.

Beside him, Jack sat in silence watching the passing countryside and Ben rode on the back strap, acting as tiger. Drew had discovered that the two brothers were as opposite as could be, and not just physically. Having crewed on many a ship with lads of the same age, Drew was used to dealing with them. But Jack was a complete enigma to the captain. Unlike the boys at sea, Jack had a quiet reserve about him that was rare. There was some mystery there, or some hurt, in Drew's opinion. As they drew closer to the end of their travels, Jack grew quieter and more remote while Ben was as lively as ever, wanting to see everything and asking a multitude of questions about their journey and about Drew's life in Calcutta.

As Drew pondered the boys' differences, he wondered if it might be usual for brothers to be different despite common parents. He wouldn't know, for his had been a lonely upbringing. Still, he felt there was some secret behind Jack's hazel eyes and he hoped that someday the boy would be comfortable enough to confide in him.

He put the Trudeau brothers' quirks from his mind as the curricle topped a rise. The villages of Westbury and Wookey came into view together, being only miles apart. He reined his vehicle to a halt on a little stone bridge with a small creek flowing gently beneath. His mind filled with long-ago memories of a time when he had cavorted in the hills and gorges of the land around Rowland with his friends from the villages, a rough and rowdy lot of whom his father had disapproved. But that was long ago. He was no longer that callow youth who'd given little thought to anything but pleasure. It was good to be home, even in such strained circumstances.

From behind him Ben called, "What are we stopped for, sir?"

"I was just envisioning the adventures of my childhood, lad. Riding to the hounds in the autumn, drinking cool cider by the River Axe on a hot summer afternoons, exploring the warm caves and grottos in Cheddar Gorge in the winter . . ." he chuckled before he added, "searching for the Witch of Wookey Cave—"

"A witch?" Ben's eyes lit with excitement. "Jack, you never told me there was a witch nearby."

"Because it's only a pile of old rocks in a very deep cave that looks like a witch," Jack said, more interested in surveying the vista than in the legend of the monk who'd turned a witch to stone.

Drew's brows rose. "You know of our witch? I wouldn't have thought our mythical old crone would be so well-known in Bristol." Jack flashed a glance his way and the captain could almost swear there was a moment of anxiety in the boy's face.

A strange thought entered Drew's mind: It was a shame that such lovely eyes were wasted on a lad, for any young girl would relish those thick, long lashes. Drew's attention dropped to the small mole at Jack's mouth and familiarity niggled at him. No doubt it reminded him of someone of little import or he would remember.

Jack's husky voice interrupted his reflections. "Every child in Somerset knows the Legend of the Wookey Witch, sir."

The lad shifted in the seat and Drew suspected Jack was deliberately avoiding his gaze. Was he scared of the legend and didn't want to admit being so? He didn't want to pursue the subject for fear they might decide to go to the very cave and look? Drew wouldn't embarrass him by pressing the matter.

Before he could change the subject, a man and a woman cantered out of the nearby woods. The horses were mediocre stock but the clothes of the riders were stylish and well cut. The faces were vaguely familiar, but Drew couldn't place their names.

The pair spotted the stopped carriage, then halted to have a brief, whispered conversation. A small tiff seemed to be brewing, then reluctantly, the young man approached, clearly at the female's urging. "Have you lost your way, sir?"

There was a sudden gasp by Jacinda. Drew turned to look at her, but she had covered her nose and mouth as if she meant to sneeze and turned her head aside.

The captain hoped the lad wasn't coming down with something, for the baron's health was rumored to be indifferent at best. Drew turned his attention back to the young gentleman. "Not lost, sir. I'd merely stopped to gaze once again on the countryside of my youth. But thank you for your query."

The elegant woman with the fiery locks beneath a black low crown beaver hat trotted up to them. Her fashionable green riding habit was done in the military style and suited her lush figure well. Her curious gaze was fixed on Drew as she spoke softly to the plump young man. "Do remember your manners and present yourself, brother."

The man shot her an annoyed look but dutifully stood in his irons. "Giles Devere at your service, sir. May I present my sister, the Widow Tyne."

The captain skillfully stood without so much as disturbing his team and doffed his black beaver hat, which he'd purchased to come into the country. "Captain Drew Morrow, ma'am, sir, on my way to Rowland Park for a long-overdue reunion with my father. I believe we met some years ago in Westbury." He resettled both his hat and position.

Shock registered on both the brother's and sister's faces. They exchanged a look before Mr. Devere sputtered out, "The baron's heir? But we heard . . . that is . . ."

Drew arched one brow. "You heard that I had murdered old Blanchett, then run away to sea and died a

tragic death as my just end?" Drew had decided that he
would face the rumors head on.

Stunned silence reigned for a moment, then Mrs.
Tyne tittered. "Good heavens, Captain, as if we ever
believed that you had anything to do with our uncle's
death. I have said all along that it was some low person who preys on travelers and it was the old gentleman's unfortunate luck to be robbed that night. Have
no fear that you won't be welcomed back to our com-
munity, *Captain* Morrow. Why, I should like to issue
an invitation to take tea at Blanchett Manor at your
earliest convenience." She looked coyly at him through
her lashes.

Giles Devere nodded his agreement as he took stock
of the gentleman's equipage and well-bred cattle, which
bespoke a sufficiency of funds not generally associated
with the Morrow name. "As my sister said, it was just a
great deal of gossip by the locals, sir. I do believe even
Prudence and I were mentioned as suspects, along with
everyone else who ever came in contact with the old
gentleman. I assure you I never believe a word of it. You
are most welcome at the manor any day." His eyes narrowed slightly as he watched his sister flutter her lashes
at the captain.

"Thank you. I should welcome an invitation." It was
a visit he intended all along in the hopes of hearing
news about the little lost heiress. But he didn't mention
the matter at present, for it might be a painful subject
for her relatives. He would inquire of the girl later.

"Then it's settled," Mrs. Tyne rushed to accept. "Tea,
say, Friday afternoon at two." Good-byes were said and
the pair rode away but not before the widow slyly added,
"I look forward to our next meeting, sir."

Beside the captain, Jacinda had quaked in fear during

the entire five-minute conversation. But she needn't have concerned herself, for neither of her cousins had so much as given her or Ben a second glance. Servants were nonentities to the likes of them except as those who did their bidding. For that, Jacinda was thankful. Considering the matter, she wasn't certain they would have recognized her as their cousin anyway since she was much changed. Gone were the pallor, the gaunt features, and the lank long hair. Perhaps what would be most surprising for Giles and Prudence in Jacinda's opinion would be her loss of timidity. Life in the ranks of the common man had taught her to stand up for herself and what she believed.

Perhaps the only thing that had struck her as strange about their inadvertent encounter was her reaction to her cousin's flirting with Captain Morrow. A peculiar anger had settled in her. Why should she care if the girl was making a cake of herself? She could only think her dislike of it was because Prudence must know the gentleman was all but betrothed to Jacinda. What could her cousin have been thinking to behave in such a fast manner? Jacinda's gaze drifted to the captain. He was very handsome.

Unaware of his companion's scrutiny, the captain urged his team to a trot. The carriage moved toward Rowland Park and, Jacinda hoped, for the truth. The next few weeks were going to be difficult, perhaps even dangerous. Discovery of her true identity might prove fatal. A tremor of fear raced up her spine as she remembered that night when those masked men had searched the rocks for her. Someone had wanted her dead and she must never forget that. She glanced at the man beside her. His strong profile was set into a frown. He appeared just as apprehensive about re-

turning home . . . but what could he have to fear? All
he faced was the welcome of the heir once again where
he belonged. Doubts about him resurfaced. Had he
been involved in her father's death? But she didn't
truly believe that. The more time she spent with him,
the less she feared him, but she promised herself not
to let her guard down until the truth was known.

Rowland Park was little changed since either of the
carriage's occupants had last seen the old manor house
eight years earlier. Like a man-made mountain, it had
withstood the progress of time as well as could be expected. The timbered surface would likely stand another
hundred years without much change, but the white-
washed stucco had yellowed and cracked in places. The
board that covered the broken front window remained
as it had been so long ago, but was now weathered to a
pale gray color. The grounds were more overgrown, the
lawn gone to seed, and the only flowers were wild ones
that had taken root in the once lovely gardens.

A sad look came over the captain's countenance at the
evidence of neglect everywhere and he shook his head.
"There's a great deal of work to do, lads." They traveled
slowly up a gravel driveway where weeds had taken root
and potholes were to be avoided. The gentleman halted
his carriage in front of the old oak entry and Ben scrambled to the horses' heads.

"Jack, come with me and I shall present you to my father's housekeeper. Hopefully there will be a place for you
on the staff." He called to Ben, "Walk the horses until I
see if my father shall welcome me home." The gentleman
climbed down and Jacinda scrambled after him, but he
stood and looked up at the manor a moment. If his fur-

rowed brows and fisted hand were any indication, he was reliving his last memories here and they weren't pleasant. Finally he went up the stone steps and rapped the knocker. There were three more tries with the lion head knocker before an ancient butler with a shock of white hair pulled the door open.

"May I—" He froze and his eyes widened. "I-is it truly you, Master Andrew?"

A grin lit the captain's face at the juvenile address. "Hodges, I'm home. Let us hope I shall be welcomed back."

The old man grew teary-eyed. "Let there be no doubt about that, sir."

"Is there a groom that can show young Ben the ropes in the stables?" The captain gestured to where the lad walked the horses down the drive.

The old servant peered at the curricle and four, and his brows rose at the sight of such prime stock. "There's been little need for any grooms since Lady Rowland sold your father's hunter this spring. There's only old Rosie that we use to bring supplies from town and to take her ladyship to church on Sunday. Seth, Cook's father, takes care of the mare."

Captain Morrow's brow wrinkled "The slow one who used to sleep in the pantry?" When Hodges nodded, the gentleman asked, "Are my father's circumstances that bleak?"

"Aye, sir, things are bad, and not just with the funds as you'll soon see." The butler shook his head. He glanced over his shoulder before he continue in a lowered tone. "The old gentleman's in a bad way what with the injuries from the fall he took and her ladyship always at him." He shrugged before he added, "But then,

I'd guess that some think she's the one what got the bad bargain."

The captain didn't continue to discuss his father's circumstances with the old family retainer on the door stoop. He gestured at Jacinda. "I've brought two lads with me. Ben will lend a hand in the stables and I'm hoping there is something Jack can do here at the house. An under footman perhaps?"

Jacinda bowed to the old man like her father's footman had to Stritch. The butler's narrowed eyes swept over her and she thought she wasn't faring well in his judgment. While she was tall for a female, she was much shorter than the average footman. For a moment she wondered if he saw through her disguise, for he frowned so frightfully.

"Sir, it's a grand thing that you've done, bringing us more help, but how your father's going to pay the lads is beyond me. There's her ladyship, to boot. She don't like anyone usurping her role in making such household decisions. Fired Mrs. Lester, she did, for hiring a parlor maid without consulting her first." The old man's brows drew inward, giving his amiable face a fierce look. Then his eyes widened. "But what am I thinking, do come in, sir."

Jacinda followed the captain into the cool, dark great hall and looked about. Her memory from her one visit was vague but even she could see things had changed. The walls had been all but stripped bare of paintings and tapestries. Gone to cover expenses, no doubt. At one end of the great hall, near the fireplace, a battered old settle and two large iron candle stands were all that decorated the huge entry.

"You needn't worry about the lads, Hodges, I shall see to their pay." Shock played on the captain's features

at the stark state of things. He looked upward at cob-
webs that hung from the iron chandeliers, then his gaze
locked on the shadows at the top of the stairs. He
bowed.

Jacinda looked up and caught sight of a tall woman
staring down at them from the upper landing. Her attire
was garish even to Jacinda's inexperienced eyes. The
bright red silk had too much lace and furbelows for an
afternoon gown.

The woman stepped forward to demand, "Hodges, who
is this and why was I not informed we had visitors?"

"Lady Rowland," there was a tired quality to the servant's voice as if he'd gotten used to such treatment,
"'tis not visitors, but the master's only son returned
from . . ." Hodges frowned, for he hadn't a clue where
the heir had been.

"From Calcutta." Captain Morrow filled in the missing information even as he took the lady's measure.

Jacinda recognized this woman's type in an instant.
London was full of such females. Rich merchants'
daughters with steely ambition, a thin veneer of breed-
ing, garish taste in apparel, and a great deal of arro-
gance. They rode about in their carriages in the poorer
parts of town, hoping to garner the respect they were denied from the gentry in Mayfair. Lady Rowland looked
to be barely thirty, which was rather startling since the
baron would be near sixty by now. She was tall and thin
with a face that might have been called handsome but
for the sour set of her thin lips.

For a moment Jacinda wondered: had her father lived
and had she remained at Chettwood, would she have become one of those types? A smile touched her lips when
Cousin Millie came to mind. Unbecoming behavior—
over that lady's dead body. She'd had a rule of conduct

for every occasion. No doubt, she would have seen to it that Jacinda behaved a proper young lady. It was the advantage of having had a mother from the upper ranks who'd employed a distant cousin to oversee her only daughter's education. Jacinda schooled her face to the placid mask of a servant.

The baroness held her position for a few minutes, almost as if to remind them who she was. Satisfied she'd made her point, she came down the stairs stopping just above their position. She looked down her nose at her new stepson. "Well, young man, it surprises me that you would show your face here after all the pain and disappointment you caused your father. I suppose you will be trying to see what you can get from him, but be warned that I shall not allow you to take advantage in my role as your new Mama."

The captain bowed a second time. "Madam, I know I have much to do to make up for my behavior. I failed my father so many years ago, but I've come to make amends for those failures if he will allow, not to ask for favors."

"Make amends? How might you do that? The little heiress is long gone so I cannot think what you might do to make up for his disappointment there." She shook her head then turned her cold gaze on Jacinda as if her stepson could have no answer.

"There are ways, madam, but I think this is something I must speak with my father about if I see—"

"Who is this low person and why is he loitering here in my hall? " Lady Rowland asked interrupting him as if he were no more important than the servant she looked at. "Your taste in companions leaves much to be desired."

A brief flash of anger in the captain's eyes disappeared quickly. Jacinda sensed a struggle within him to maintain his temper.

"This is Jack. I brought him with me to Rowland Park, for I owe him a great debt and hoped to find employment for him on the estate."

"A debt? Why am I not surprised? In that respect you are like your father. I won't have ruffians in my house. I suppose we could use him in the gardens. I understand the old gardener's cottage is empty since he died, not that I ever saw evidence that he did much work his final years. All his tools must still be in the shed. The boy can fill that position."

Jacinda's heart sank. The surrounding grounds looked as if they hadn't seen a hoe, a scythe, or shears in years. The formal gardens appeared even worse. Then she flashed on an old memory of wonderful hours with her mother and the gardener at Chettwood, working side by side. She had listened to old Hatfield's advice to her mother about planting, pruning, and other suggestions. Jacinda felt certain she could transform the tangled, overgrown mess outside into a thing of beauty. And best of all, she would have no one looking over her shoulder, as Lady Rowland didn't look like a woman who paid much heed to such things. Jacinda's position would give her a great deal of time to pursue her true reason for being there. She tugged her hat politely and said, "Thank you, ma'am."

"Hodges," Lady Rowland spoke the butler's name as if he'd disappointed her on more than one occasion, "Take the boy in hand and show him what his tasks shall be." She then turned her sour gaze on Jacinda. "And don't think I won't fire you, boy, if I don't see proper progress."

Jacinda bowed. "Yes, ma'am."

When she moved to follow the butler, Captain Morrow turned and winked at her. "I'll speak with you later, Jack. You and Ben settle into the gardener's cottage and I'll have Cook send down some supper."

"Who is Ben?" Her ladyship folded her hands in front of her and arched one brow. "More debt, sir?"

"Ben is Jack's brother, and he shall do nicely helping Seth in the stables. You needn't fear the expense, madam, Ben is my tiger."

Jacinda followed the butler through the green baize door. The last thing she heard was the captain asking to see his father before the butler's voice interrupted, telling her what would be expected of her. She was taken below stairs and introduced to the staff, which were few. There were Cook, two maids, a footman, Lord Rowland's valet, and, of course, Hodges, none of whom were under fifty years of age. Hoping to make inroads into their good will, Jacinda offered to do any errands the staff might need when she wasn't occupied with the grounds. The plump upstairs maid pinched the lad's cheek and declared "Jack" to be pretty as a girl, with skin just as soft and manners to boot.

Jacinda gave her best scowl and merely declared, "Give me a few years. I'm only fourteen." It was the only way to explain her lack of whiskers and delicate features.

After some further teasing, the footman, whose name was Nate, lead her out to the tiny cottage in the woods behind the stables, all the while chattering gossip about the family. She was quick to determine that the servants thought the estate was rather adrift with no steward and the baron abed. The only thing she found of interest was that Nate warned her to steer clear of Lady Rowland. "She's little better than a fishmonger wife in lace, but no pearls, them was sold for the money. And she got a tongue what runs on wheels when she's in the boughs."

Nate brought her to a small stone cottage. She could see a pond in the rear woods. "Tools are in a shed in the back and I'm guessin' her ladyship will give the rest of the day to rest 'afore she expects ye to work." On that dark note, he left her.

It was a plain stone cottage with primroses growing up the walls. She opened the door and went inside. There was a small, single room with a sooty hearth and a tiny loft. It was bigger than most of the rooms she and Ben had lived in the last few years, but not by much. There were several pieces of furniture: a table, two chairs, a cupboard, and a rough-hewn bed frame that stood in the corner with a feather mattress rolled and bound on the rope slats. She would get Ben to help her roll it out for airing along with the one she could see in the loft.

She moved to the lone window, which overlooked a pasture. The daisies and cowslips growing wild reminded her of Chettwood and she remembered just how close she was to her old life. Her father's manor was only five miles away. She pulled her mother's locket from beneath her shirt and fingered it tenderly. She always wore it to remind her of all that she had lost and of what she needed to do. But Chettwood might as well be a hundred miles away, for she would have a great deal of work to do here . . . at least until she showed enough progress that no one would question her about her ability.

Still, she suspected that in her position as gardener she would have a great deal of leeway in doing her work. As far as her investigation into her father's murder, she would need to take things slowly. It would never do to have her masquerade end too soon by discovery that she was not only a female, but the heiress to the Blanchett fortune. With a determined sigh, she tucked the locket safely away and set about cleaning the cottage in which she and Ben would now live.

Ben arrived some thirty minutes later with their meager belongings, which he set beside the door as he inspected their new living quarters.

At last he pulled out a chair, settled himself, and gave Jacinda a piercing stare. "Are you going to finally explain to me why we've come back to the very place where someone tried to kill you?"

She pulled out the chair opposite and sat down. "Ben, I'm tired of living in fear. I'm tired of being poor and hungry. It's time for me to learn the truth. To find the murderer of my father."

The boy sat up straight. "But that could be dangerous, Jack. Do. . . do you think they will still want to harm you?"

"Without a doubt." She spoke the words casually but her insides were in knots at the prospect of anyone learning that she was Jacinda Blanchett and not Jack Trudeau.

Ben's brows drew together. "We can't do this alone; we shall need help. Who can we trust here?"

"No one, Ben, no one but each other."

"But I'd swear the captain—"

"Not even Captain Morrow, Ben. If he learns the truth he will feel duty-bound to make me return home. Besides, I cannot even be certain that he wasn't involved that night."

The boy didn't look happy, but he nodded his understanding. He got up and came to her, taking her hands. "Only promise me, Jack, that you'll be careful. You're all I have left."

She ruffled his hair. "I promise."

* * *

Drew stepped into the large room after a weak voice called for him to enter. Lord Rowland's chambers lay in near darkness. Heavy green curtains were drawn against the daylight, and two candles flickered on either side of the four-post bed. The small flames added to the heat and stuffiness of the enclosed room and the soft light did little to mask the shabbiness of the draperies. The baron's skin was drawn tightly over his pale face, his body a frail memory of the once robust gentleman.

"Hello, Father." As shocked as Drew was at the physical change in his father, what worried him most was the apathy in the old gentleman's eyes even on seeing his only son again. No joy or surprise, not even anger registered in the depths of his dark eyes. It was almost as if the life had already gone out of him. Guilt again surfaced inside Drew. Had *he* done this to his father?

"Andrew?" The old gentleman's voice sounded weak but the first hint of welcome lay in that one word.

Drew took the frail hand in his, but his father merely continued to stare. There was little doubt in Drew's mind that it was up to him to break the ice, but he didn't know where to start. At last he said the only thing he could think to say. "Father, can you ever forgive me?"

The old man sighed and shook his head then stared off into space. The rejection tore at Drew's insides. The baron's next words weren't what Drew expected. "It doesn't matter, boy. All my plans would have been scotched even if you'd been here. Nothing went as I thought. You disappeared, Blanchett's dead, that sickly little girl's still missing, I haven't a feather to fly with and I took an immoderate shrew for a wife. None of it matters any more." He'd closed his eyes as if those few words were too much for him and his energy was spent.

"It does matter, sir. I want to make things right. I can make things right both here and with Miss Blanchett."

Drew saw the first spark of interest from his father since he'd entered the room. "How?"

"Most important will be to put Rowland Park to rights and to get you from that bed."

Lord Rowland gave a bitter chuckle. "It would take a great deal of money for the first and only God could do the second."

"I've been told the doctor says you can walk if only you will try. As to the other, I have money, sir. It's taken eight years, but I have made my fortune and I fully intend to invest it here, in my home, if you still consider me your heir."

"Of course you are my heir." The baron grew silent as he contemplated his son's words. "You are still obligated to that girl. There's nothing we can do about her, for I signed those papers the night you disappeared, albeit I didn't know you'd run off until later. But it's all moot, for very likely the poor thing is dead and buried."

"I intend to find out, sir. I'll hire someone to look for her and her maid. I'll start with Blanchett's lawyer. He claims to be receiving letters from her. If she's alive, I'll find her, Father, and when I do I'll honor your wishes and marry her. Rowland Park and Chettwood Manor will become one estate, just as you planned."

For a moment the baron seemed to take heart from his son's words, then his gaze dropped to his legs hidden under the bed linens and the spark of light seemed to go out. "It doesn't matter. I shall never leave this bed. Do what you will."

Both his father's solicitor and his stepmother had told Drew that the doctor had said the old gentleman could walk again, but he would have to want to do it. It was too early to hope for any changes. If he could make things better then his father's spirits might improve. Drew would take one endeavor at a time and for now that would be working to restore the estate.

"Very well, sir, if I must then I shall do things alone, but I would much prefer to have my father at my side. I shall begin first thing in the morning by hiring a new steward." With that he left his father, hoping that something he'd said had rekindled his father's spirit.

CHAPTER FOUR

"Let go, you ugly blighter." Jacinda tugged at the stubborn weed which stood nearly waist high. The borders along the walk in Rowland Park's east garden had been full of such weeds when she'd first started. Now they were heaped in a large pile for Ben to haul off later. After most of the morning pulling them, her strength was almost spent. She gave one last tug and the roots suddenly pulled from the ground, causing Jacinda to tumble backward. She landed hard on her backside in the newly scythed grass and her hat flew off. She chuckled and lay back to rest for a moment, enjoying the warm sunshine and the smell of honeysuckle on the nearby stone wall that sheltered the garden from the wind.

After three days of backbreaking work, the results of her efforts were beginning to show. This one garden was almost back to what it had been twenty years earlier. She knew because Nate had shown her a watercolor that had been painted by a former guest of the Park's gardens during it's heyday. A series of three pictures hung in the hallway where the servants came and went. Jacinda stopped and stared at them each morning when she and Ben came for breakfast with the servants. It gave her an idea of what she was striving for as a final result.

Exhausted, she savored the moment in the grass with her eyes closed. Her back hurt, her hands were blistered and—her eyes popped open when she heard a footfall in the gravel walk beside her. She stared up into the smiling face of Captain Morrow.

"Are we working you too hard, Jack?" He smiled down at her.

Jacinda scrambled to her feet. "N-no, sir. I just fell backwards while pulling weeds." She lifted the offending plant still clutched in her hand, then tossed it to the weed pile to her left. Her gaze swept over the captain. This morning he looked different somehow. They hadn't met since the night they'd first arrived, so perhaps her imagination was playing tricks on her. Her gaze swept over him a second time. He definitely looked different.

Seth had told them the gentleman was so busy what with hiring a new steward and going over the books, he'd scarcely left the library, going so far as to have his meals served there, a fact that had piqued Lady Rowland. But fatigue wasn't what made him appear different. A soft breeze wafted through the garden and the scent of lavender and spice tickled her nose. Then she realized what had changed. He'd cut his hair into a more fashionable style. A Brutus, was it called? Also, his clothes were much more fashionable than the buckskins and driving coat he'd worn to drive down. Why, he looked as if he were going somewhere important.

Noting the direction of her gaze, the gentleman self-consciously ran a hand through the neatly arranged style, mussing it a bit, then tugged at his waistcoat. "My father's valet insisted he must see to me. Is it dreadful?"

Jacinda could only stare for a moment for, if anything, it made him more handsome. The dark gray jacket over a light gray waistcoat complemented his emerald eyes. The elegance of his cravat would rival any gentleman in Town and his once mud-stained Hessians shone like mirrors in the sunlight. "No, no, it is very stylish, sir. You will turn all the ladies heads." A thought that strangely did little to please her.

The captain reach out and tweaked a blade of grass from her unruly curls. "If you like I shall have Clark trim your hair, as well. If your mane gets much longer, lad, they'll be mistaking you for a girl in town with that baby face."

Jacinda's heart sank and she scrambled to recover her hat, which she then pulled down low over her face. "That won't be necessary, Captain. Ben and I trim each other's hair." She promised herself to trim it at the earliest possible moment. "Was there something you wanted, sir?"

Morrow turned and surveyed the garden where they stood. "You have been doing an excellent job, Jack. I've seen Ben helping from the library windows. Speaking of which, where is the lad? I stopped by the stables to order my carriage and he wasn't there."

"There just aren't enough horses to keep Ben busy what with Seth, too, so my brother's lending a hand here. He's burning leaves and grass in a pit behind the barn, sir. Seth said that was how the old gardener did it."

"Very good. What I came to tell you is I think there is too much for you to do alone or even with Ben's help. You look exhausted. Take the rest of the afternoon off. Have Seth saddle Rosie. I should like you to ride into Westbury and see Mr. Samford at the Samford Arms. Tell him Lord Rowland is looking for, say, three sturdy lads to work at the Park during the day. We shall need them to start on Monday. I would handle it myself, but I am promised to tea with Mrs. Tyne and her brother this afternoon at Chettwood."

A strange coil of jealousy stirred in Jacinda's chest. She had completely forgotten the invitation. *She* should be the one welcoming the captain to her home, not her cousin. Noting the twinkle in his eyes, curiosity got the better of her and she couldn't resist asking, "Are you . . . taken with the widow, sir?"

The gentleman's brows rose. "I hardly know her and it really wouldn't matter if I were 'taken with the lady,' as you call it, Jack." Captain Morrow eyes grew distant as his thoughts seemed to grow dark. "I am duty-bound to marry her cousin. No, I'm merely happy to be out of the house for the afternoon."

There was a part of her that was pleased, and yet not. She was glad that he wasn't smitten but why would he pursue a marriage that he'd so adamantly opposed at sixteen? Jacinda probed further. "Her cousin? Why, sir?"

The gentleman shook his head. "It's a long, ugly story, lad. All I shall tell you is that long ago I made a mistake and did Miss Blanchett a terrible wrong. I shall do what I can to make up for it by doing my duty to the child. But you don't want to hear about my troubles. We can discuss how you fare in Westbury on my return." On that he turned and strode off to the stables.

A hollow feeling settled over Jacinda. What wrong had he done her? Killed her father? Failed to stop his father from doing such a crime? She still wouldn't believe he'd had a hand there, but that was only part of her pain. He would marry her without caring a fig for

her, all because of duty and honor. It made her feel
sick inside. She had already been through enough in
her life. She was no longer that frail little girl who
would have done what her father wanted. When she
was once again in her place at Chettwood, she would
release him from the betrothal and send him away.
She didn't want an unwilling husband.

A wave of desolation swept over her. She might
never find someone who would love her for anything
but her money. Her spine stiffened and she held her
head higher. She was strong, and she would face whatever the future held even if Captain Morrow was to
be no part of that.

She seemed to assume that he had no involvement in
her father's death. Perhaps it was only that she didn't
want it to be so, for she had come to like the gentleman.
He was everything one could admire, having fought
back from nothing to earn his own fortune.

With a sigh she picked up the weeds and hauled them
to where Ben was working. She ordered him to stay near
the fire until it was completely out, then told him of her
mission to town. He begged her to bring him a treat, and
she promised she would if possible. There had been few
such treats in his young life.

Seth had already spoken with the captain, who'd
left for Chettwood only minutes before she arrived,
and a saddled horse awaited. She washed her hands
and face in the horse trough and climbed up onto the
mare's back.

It had been years since she'd ridden but it was a skill
that one didn't forget. She jogged along on Rosie, enjoying her free afternoon. Within ten minutes of leaving
Rowland Park she trotted past the gates of Chettwood.
A lump formed in her throat as she stared up the drive.

The house wasn't visible. It sat too far back from the road, but she knew the captain was there even now, having tea with Prudence and Giles as well as Aunt Devere and Cousin Millie. It made her feel melancholy.

She slumped in the saddle, letting her mind dwell on what it would be like to see everyone she knew again. To own the truth, even Millie's overprotectiveness wouldn't seem so bad to her after all these years.

Realizing that it was getting late, Jacinda urged Rosie into a canter towards the village. Another fifteen minutes of riding and the horse rounded a curve where the village of Westbury came into view. A lump formed in her throat when memories of coming here with her mother overwhelmed her. Then a moment of fear beset her when several people stared at her. It took a moment for her to realize they only did so out of curiosity at a stranger arriving in their small village.

At last she spied the Samford Arms and guided the animal into the inn yard. She climbed down and gave her horse over to an ostler. Once inside, the innkeeper, Mr. Samford, was clearly skeptical when she first mentioned hiring lads for Rowland Park. Once she convinced him *Captain Morrow* was returned and determined to set the estate to rights, the old proprietor's eyes gleamed.

"So, young Morrow is back and plump in the pockets? I wonder how long that will last once the baron is back on his feet and back to his old ways." A wicked gleam settled in the old man's eyes. "I reckon the squire's daughter will be wanting the captain to call again." The old gentleman chuckled.

Jacinda frowned. "The squire's daughter?"

"Aye, as memory serves, the lad was mad for Mariah Amberly. Only she's Lady Bancroft these days, not but what the earl ever notices. He's seventy if he's a day."

With that the innkeeper called to his wife to send for his son and for the blacksmith's lads as well, for there was money to be made.

Jacinda recalled that a youthful Morrow had spoken of a Mariah that day in the hallway. He'd professed himself in love with her. Yet, she had married someone else. Did the captain still have feelings for her?

Three burly lads arrived and turned Jacinda's mind to the matter at hand. It seemed very strange for her to be directing such large lads but they were more interested in the money than her presumed age. A sum was agreed to and they all promised to be at the estate by six o'clock Monday morning.

With her business complete, she strolled the streets of town, looking in the shop windows. At last she came to a mercantile, where she bought Ben a couple of pieces of hard candy. That done, she retrieved Rosie and set out to return to the Park.

She pressed the old mare into a canter, but as she neared the gates of Chettwood, the old draw to see the place got the better of her. She reined the horse and stopped in the road, staring at the empty driveway. She wanted to see it up close and if she were careful, it would hurt nothing. The servants should be busy this late in the day preparing for supper and all her relations would be resting or changing for the evening meal.

With a swift glance in both directions, she urged Rosie through the gates of her old home. A few feet in, she veered off the main drive and trotted thought the woods. Her destination was an old tree that grew beside the walled garden that her mother had had built. She came to the small stream that ran across the side of the property. After tying Rosie to a tree, Jacinda set out on a footpath that the servants used to go back and forth to the village.

Within minutes she came to the open field in which the grounds were set. She spied the tree, much larger after eight years of growth. Long branches dipping close to the ground would make it all the easier to climb. Crossing the open field to get to it would be risky, but there didn't seem to be anyone about. She dashed over the open ground and quickly scrambled up the branches to the top of the wall. The air caught in her lungs as she looked over the wall into the garden. It was just as she remembered it. The roses were in full bloom, their sweet scent soft on the breeze, the shrubs were neatly trimmed, and the fountain gurgled happily just like on the last day she'd walked there. Whoever was in charge since her father had died had done an excellent job of maintaining the estate. Her eyes welled with tears. She missed her old home. Despite all her fears, she did want to return, and that meant she must begin to ask questions . . . but how?

A face suddenly appeared in an upstairs window. Jacinda ducked down, fearful of being seen, and her foot slipped off the limb. Despite her attempt to grab a branch, she fell. The tree limbs battered her all the way down, but thankfully helped break her fall. She hit the ground hard. Dust swirled around her, making it difficult to breathe. Or perhaps the wind had been knocked from her. For a moment she lay there gasping, fanning dust from her face. After the cloud settled she took a moment to test her limbs, nothing seemed broken, still the fall—

"Ye there, lad, just what do ye think ye're doing here?" A female voice called from behind her.

Jacinda struggled to her feet. A difficult task, since

everything on her ached. She turned away from the voice, afraid someone might recognize her. Not wanting a confrontation with any of her father's servants, she began to limp back up the path away from the garden. She called over her shoulder in her best imitation of a farm lad. "Sorry, miss, I lost me way 'ome."

But the woman was not so easily duped. She lifted her skirts and hurried after Jacinda. The servant caught up with her in the middle of the field. "Here now, what nonsense is this? I saw ye in that tree." She grabbed Jacinda's arm and spun her around. "Yer up to no good, lad. Ye was in that tree lookin' in the garden. Or are ye come to visit one of them silly parlor maids?"

Jacinda recognized the woman at once as her mother's former maid, Martha. She had stayed on after her mother's death to work for the other ladies of the household.

"Speak up, lad, I'll not—" Martha froze midsentence. She reached out and clutched something at Jacinda's chest.

To her horror, the fall had caused her mother's locket to come out of her shirt. There could be little doubt that Martha recognized the distinctive piece of jewelry that held two interlocking hearts with rubies. It had been a wedding gift from her father, a surprisingly affecting gift for a man who strayed so often.

Martha's gaze swept over the face only inches from hers and she opened her mouth as if to accuse the lad of heaven knew what, but then she locked on the tiny mole at the edge of the stranger's full mouth. "Oh, saints in heaven! God has answered our prayers. Is it ye, Miss Jacinda?" She pulled a handkerchief from her apron pocket and began to wipe dust from the girl's face.

"Look at ye, so grown up, so healthy . . . and so very dirty. Why Miss Millie will—"

Jacinda grabbed her hands. "You mustn't tell my cousin I'm here, Martha."

Doubt played over the older woman's face for a moment, then she shrugged and folded Jacinda into her ample arms. She hugged the girl until Jacinda thought her ribs would break. "Martha, you must promise me not to tell a soul that I am here in Somerset. They would make me come home."

The maid drew back. "Ye ain't here to stay?"

"It's not safe for me until my father's murderer is found."

"Oh!" Martha caressed Jacinda's face, still dabbing with her handkerchief at dirty spots. "I was so delighted to see ye alive and well that I didn't think of that. Where's Trudy, miss?"

Despite the tightening in her throat, Jacinda was able to speak. "Dear Trudy died years ago, but she made certain I was in the safekeeping of her family. I'm staying in the neighborhood at present and my safety depends on keeping my identity a secret. I've come home to learn the truth, and I could use your help."

"I'll do anything ye need, miss. Ye've only to ask." Martha stared at the face that was much changed, then, overwhelmed with joy, she leaned over and showered kisses on Jacinda's cheeks. "It's so wonderful that yer alive, child."

Delighted to feel so welcome, Jacinda embraced the woman. After a moment she begged the old servant to tell her everything that had happened at Chettwood since she'd left. Martha looked over her shoulder at the manor, then slid her arm round Jacinda's waist and led her towards the woods. "Someone might see us out here, miss. Come with me. There's a good deal I can tell you about what's been happenin'."

As the pair disappeared into the woods, they were unaware their encounter had been observed. Drew Morrow sat with his hands on the reins of his carriage, about to depart from Chettwood Manor where he'd stayed overlong, hoping to glean information about Miss Blanchett and the progress on solving the murder. He'd seen the lad appear, hurrying across the field. At first he'd almost glanced away, but there was something so familiar about the boy he stared harder. It was quite a distance from where the captain sat, but he recognized Jack Trudeau's slender form and that huge floppy hat the lad always wore. Drew's first thought was to wonder if the boy had come to bring him a message, but if that were so then why would Jack not have come to the front door? So what was he doing at Chettwood?

Within minutes of Jack's appearance, a slender female of indeterminate age hurried up behind him. Drew watched, wondering what was about to happen, for the woman seemed to be confronting Jack. A cold feeling settled into Drew's gut. He knew little about the two lads he'd brought to his home. They'd saved him, and he had been so grateful that he hadn't questioned their integrity. But he could only think of one reason for the boy to come to a strange house in a neighborhood he wasn't familiar with. Had Jack been a housebreaker in London?

To Drew's utter surprise, the woman began to kiss Jack, then within minutes she hugged the lad, who in turn embraced her as well. What was this? Was the boy some kind of infant Romeo? Drew watched in amazement as the woman slid an arm round the lad's waist and led him into the woods.

Drew stared at the place where the pair disappeared through the trees for several minutes before he finally told his horse to walk on. It didn't surprise him that females would swoon for such a pretty lad, but Jack was scarcely dry behind the ears. It had to be something else that had brought the lad here . . . but what?

A myriad of possibilities went through Drew's head and none of them were good. As he swept out the gates of Chettwood, he promised to speak with the boy at the first opportunity. At present he was going to see his father's doctor to find out what could be done to motivate him to leave his bed. Casting one final glance in the direction the pair in the field had gone, Drew frowned. He didn't need Jack causing trouble in Chettwood. Drew needed to gain the family's confidence if he were going to root out a murderer and bring Miss Blanchett home.

Ben stirred the pot of lamb stew that Nate had brought to the cottage for their evening meal, then put the lid back and pushed the spar where the pot hung back over the low fire. He eyed the wooden spoon, then glanced around to make sure no one else was around. Having food readily available for the taking wasn't something he was used to. With a grin he licked off the thick gravy, savoring Cook's skills. He liked it at Rowland Park. The captain had seen to their every comfort. Ben's gaze roved over the room which held several comfortable chairs, blankets, and linens as well as candles and books for them to read. And not that dull, dry preachy stuff but grand stories like *Ivanhoe* and *Gulliver's Travels*.

He jumped when the door opened and Jacinda entered. "What took you—" the lad halted as he took in her grimy face and clothes. There was dirt from the top of her head to the sole of her thick boots. A grin split his mouth and he asked, "What happened to you? Take a tumble from old Rosie?"

"I fell from a tree at Chettwood." Jacinda took off her hat and beat the dust from the brim.

The smile disappeared from Ben's face. He came to her, his young face a study in fear. "I told you it was too dangerous for us to come back here. We're not here a week and already you found danger. I know I never truly believed your story, but I've asked Seth some questions and I know everything you told me is true. Someone tried to kill you, and you go to the very place where you might be recognized." A frown puckered the boy's face. "Seth also said there are people here in the village that think it might have been the captain and his father who were involved."

Jacinda tossed her hat down on the table. "That's nothing but idle gossip, Ben." She shrugged out of her jacket and walked back to the open door and shook the dust out. She didn't know why she felt the need to defend the captain. "The truth is there are plenty of people who might have wanted us dead. People who would inherit the estate." She didn't know who that entailed; since her father had warned her never to allow Mr. Wilkins to know her location, there had been only her letters to him.

"I just don't think we should be here at Rowland Park, of all places, Jack. If the baron or . . ." His voice trailed off. It was obvious he liked Captain Morrow and didn't want to think of him as a villain.

She hung her coat on a peg, then went to the boy, putting both hands on his shoulders. "Don't worry. The captain doesn't have a clue who I am. I'm safe as long as I'm just the baron's gardener. The good news is that I have an ally at Chettwood. Martha, my mother's maid, knows who I am and she'll tell us what is happening over there."

"Can you trust her?" Doubt hovered in his eyes.

"Of course. She would have had nothing to gain by my death."

As they stood looking at each other, Ben's stomach growled. They both laughed. Jacinda patted her clothes and dust swirled to the floor. "I think I need to go to the pond to have a good wash, is supper ready?"

"Whenever you are. I'll set the table while you wash but don't be long. Or I'll wait like one dog waits for another." He grinned at her and she took his meaning, which was that he wouldn't wait.

She opened a cabinet and took out her one luxury, a bar of French milled soap that she'd brought from London. Grabbing a towel, she headed out to the small spring-fed pond in the woods. She was looking forward to the cool, refreshing waters.

At the pond, she stood for a moment, taking in the beauty of the remote little clearing. The spring bubbled down the rocks into the pool, which was perhaps fifteen feet wide and three or four feet deep. On the south side, a tiny waterfall splashed into a stream where the hill sloped downward. The narrow little stream meandered into the forest and joined up with the River Axe at some distant point beyond the boundaries of the estate. Their little pond was almost a quarter mile from the cottage, much further from the manor house.

Seth had told them that the gardener had used it as his well and bath. It was quite the luxury for her after years of washing up in bowls in the tiny rooms in London. She usually waited until dark, but today she was too tired to worry. She leaned over the edge of the water to wet the soap, but as she did a puff of dust floated from her hair. She bit at her lip a moment, looked around and decided she was quite alone. She would risk a full bath.

She took off her waistcoat and gave it a good shaking, as well as her shirt. But the cuffs and collar were so grimy she decided to wash the shirt then and there. She kept glancing over her shoulder for she was too exposed with only the muslin binding covering her breasts. Within minutes the shirt was hung upon a bush to dry.

She looked at the water, then at her dusty breeches, but she was afraid to disrobe any further. She hung her mother's locket on a branch and put her boots and stockings on a rock, then waded in, the cold water biting at her skin through the clothes. It took only a few minutes for her to adjust to the water and it felt wonderful. She took her soap and washed her hair and skin until it smelled of lavender. It had been years since she'd felt this clean. At last, she climbed out and stretched out on a rock to dry in the late afternoon sun. The warm rays dried her exposed shoulders, but the layers of muslin binding her chest remained damp. She could remove it back at the cabin and allow it to dry during the night before she needed it again in the morning.

Jacinda ran her fingers through her hair, hating that she would have to cut it again for her role. As a warm breeze wafted though the glen, tousling the drying curls, she wondered if it would look like her mother's had when it was again long. Her mother's hair had been beautiful. Jacinda leaned over the water and looked at her reflection. It was much changed from that little girl so many years earlier. Her face had filled out and become healthy. Her skin glowed, as did her eyes, and her mouth curved upward with pink full lips. Perhaps she would never be a beauty, but—

"Jack?"

Startled, Jacinda fell headfirst into the pond. She stood up and through streams of water in her eyes found herself staring at Captain Morrow. An obviously shocked captain. As she followed the direction of his gaze, she looked down to see that the water had turned the thin muslin almost transparent. Her breasts were perfectly outlined in the wet fabric. Horrified, she crossed her arms in front of her and stared at the gentleman, who appeared to be in equal shock.

"Come out of the water!" he commanded.

A tremor of fear raced though her. Everything she'd planned for was lost. He would know the truth and force her to return to Chettwood where her life would become a nightmare. With a sigh she waded out of the water.

When she reached a spot in front of the gentleman, he grabbed her shirt from the bush and handed it to her. "Put this on and then I should like an explanation about this," he gestured at the male attire, "and about what you were doing at Chettwood Manor with that servant today."

She turned her back and closed her eyes as she shrugged into the wet shirt, buttoning it slowly her mind raced. What she could do or say? He was on the verge of learning the truth. She had to do everything in her power to prevent that. Gathering her wits, at last she turned back to see the puzzlement in his eyes. She must give him as little information as possible.

"What do you want to know that isn't fully obvious?" She glared at him and held onto the hope that while he knew her to be a girl, he wouldn't realize she was Jacinda Blanchett. "As to the visit to Chettwood, our grandfather was once employed there." Which was true, in fact; Ben had been named for the old groom who'd worked for her father.

"Why are you masquerading as a lad?" His gaze was riveted on her face. She turned to the right, hoping that in profile he would be less likely to recognize her. She had changed greatly, but there was still that distinctive little mole.

"I do it to take care of Ben and me. What do you think I could have done in London as a female to support us after our father disappeared?" She glanced at him and was uncomfortable with the way he was staring at her. Thinking that distance was the best strategy, she decided to leave. "What does it matter anyway? We will go back to London at once." She gathered up her shoes and waistcoat. She grabbed the locket and shoved it in her coat pocket.

"That won't be necessary. I still owe you a debt. You must give me time to think."

But Jacinda didn't want him to think. "We want to return to Town—" she pushed past him, but the captain reached out and grabbed her shoulders and turned her to face him.

He shook her, more to make his point than to hurt her, but his words were angry. "Did you not hear me? Don't be in such a rush. I owe you a debt and I fully intend to pay that debt, be it to a lad or a female. Stop being so pigheaded and listen. You won't go until we have—"

Suddenly a dark shape hurtled out of the woods. It slammed into Captain Morrow, knocking him to the ground. It was Ben, with a broom in his hands that he wielded like a weapon. He stood between the man and the woman and railed, "I won't let you hurt Jacinda!"

The name seemed to echo in the woods for a moment.

The captain sat up. "Jacinda!" A dawning look came over his features. "You are Jacinda Blanchett?" His gaze roved over her face and he seemed unable to connect that sickly child with the young woman before him.

Jacinda closed her eyes. How could she be mad at Ben? He'd only tried to defend her, but the masquerade was up, at least as far as the captain was concerned.

Captain Morrow stood and Ben raised the broom handle. "I won't let you kill her."

"Kill her? Good God, lad, what would make you think I wanted to kill her? I've been looking for her so I can marry her."

"To get her money." The lad's eyes glowed with anger.

"No, Ben. Does it look as if I need someone's money? I own the *Flying Dragon,* I'm not a cursed fortune hunter." The anger in the gentleman's eyes matched the boy's.

Ben cast a befuddled look at Jacinda, then back at the captain. "Seth said the villagers think you were involved in her father's murder."

"I was onboard a ship in Bristol by five o'clock on that dreadful day. I didn't know any of this until I returned from Calcutta two weeks ago." He looked from the lad to Jacinda. "Miss Blanchett, I swear to you I know nothing of your father's murder." A frown settled on his face. "Is that why you came back to Somerset with me? To look for your father's killer?"

Jacinda hesitated a moment, then gave a nod of her head.

"Have you taken leave of your senses? You are more likely to get yourself killed than to learn anything." He took a step towards her, and this time Ben didn't offer any threat.

There was genuine concern in the captain's eyes. It

warmed her heart. "Not if everyone thinks I'm just your gardener. Only you and I and Ben will know the truth if you let me continue in my role."

"And Martha," Ben reminded.

"Who is Martha?" Morrow looked from the boy to Jacinda.

"My mother's maid. That was who I was speaking with at Chettwood this afternoon." Seeing the doubt in the gentleman's face she added, "She can be trusted, sir, she has known me for years. She will tell us what is happening there."

The captain shook his head, but whether from shock that she'd gone to her old home or to refuse her request to remain as the gardener was unclear. Before he could speak, Ben urged, "Please, sir. She deserves to be back at Chettwood Manor where she rightfully belongs, and it won't be safe unless the killer has been captured. Let us stay here while we look for the villain."

Drew Morrow looked from one pleading face to another. How could he allow this gently bred slip of a girl to continue to do manual labor in his gardens? Yet, how could he subject her to the danger that would be hers if she returned to Chettwood with her father's killer still out there and presumably still wanting her dead? There had to be another way. He was torn as to what to do. He'd had the very woman he needed right under his nose for a week and had had no clue.

Still for the present, he had her here, and she was willing to stay as long as he continued to allow her to pretend to be a gardener. If he tried to force her back into skirts, she would likely run and everything would be back to the old stalemate.

"Very well, you may continue as you are until we come up with a better plan. But," he held up his finger to silence their protests, "I want your promise not to return to Chettwood alone. It's too dangerous."

There was rebellion in Jacinda's hazel eyes, but after a moment's contemplation the look faded. "Very well, I promise."

The glen was growing dark so Drew ordered, "Go back to the cottage before you catch your death of cold, Miss Blanchett. We'll discuss matters in the morning. Ben, take care of her."

There was an angry spark in the lady's eyes. It was obvious she was not used to being the one taken care of, but she offered no response. She walked up the path, her head held high and her back ramrod-stiff.

"I'll do that, captain." The lad saluted Drew and followed after Jacinda.

"Lord Rowland wishes to see you at once, sir." Clark, the valet, bowed and left the dining room.

Drew, lost in thought about having discovered Jacinda Blanchett under his very nose, blinked and looked about. He'd barely touched his supper. Lady Rowland had dined and left without so much as a word to him. Despite his efforts to try and be polite, theirs was not a friendly relationship. Perhaps she'd taken offence at all the missed meals but, in truth, he'd been too busy with estate matters to think about food. She'd resorted to a rather frosty silence, which he couldn't deny he preferred to her incessant criticism.

Much of his evening had been spent pondering how he'd been so blind. There had been moments over the course of the past week that he'd though "Jack" a rather delicate boy, but never had he questioned the lad's gender. Perhaps it was because there were too many such fragile lads in the teeming masses of most large cities, who were ill-fed or sickly to make one suspect a willowy boy with a pretty face was anything other than what he professed to be.

That, and the fact that Miss Blanchett made a rather plucky lad. She'd helped with their rescue from the Press Gang, endured the mad dash through the streets of London, and survived the terrors of the warehouse roof. Who would have ever suspected game young Jack to be the fragile child they'd all last seen eight years earlier?

The problem was what to do with her while they figured out the mystery of who wanted her dead. Logic told him that the murderer had to be someone after her fortune; this was why so many people suspected him and his father. He knew himself innocent and was fairly certain his father was as well, for there was no profit for them with Blanchett and his daughter gone. Which meant he could concentrate on her relatives. His thoughts returned to the tea he'd attended that afternoon.

Mrs. Devere, Giles, Mrs. Tyne, and the cousin, Miss Markham, had been present. Mrs. Tyne had been polite but openly flirtatious while her mother questioned him about his successes in Calcutta. Devere had been sullen and resentful, but whether because of his sister's immodest conduct or some grievance with Drew was uncertain. Only Miss Markham had greeted him with hostility. She seemed to blame him for the catastrophe that had befallen the family, and she'd barely spoken with him throughout his visit. She'd even rebuffed his request for information on the search for her missing cousin. Somehow he couldn't see sending Jack—no, Miss Blanchett—back into that house.

But he couldn't leave her out in the gardener's cottage while they searched for the truth. That could take months and, like Ben, Drew knew she deserved to be back in her rightful place or at least someplace safe and appropriate—which the gardener's cottage wasn't. But bringing her into the manor house here at the Park might cause even more speculation about his father and him if the truth were discovered.

Drew was at standstill. The long clock in the hall chimed the hour of eight, reminding him that his father was waiting and it was getting late. The summons was something of a surprise, for he'd not heard a word from the old gentleman despite the fact that he'd daily informed Clark of what was happening with the estate in the hopes the servant would convey the information to his father. It was an inspiration that had come to him on the first night after seeing how defeated the baron had seemed. The old gentleman's desk had been full of notes for improvements that the former bailiff had left but that his father had vetoed, mostly due to lack of funds. But it occurred to him that some of the refusals were due merely to the gentleman's resistence to change. What better way to get his father's blood up than to institute all the changes that he'd previously forbidden. In fact, most of them had seemed good modernization methods for the property.

Drew rose from the dining room and hurried up the stairs to his father's rooms. He knocked and entered to find the chamber well lit that evening. He hoped that was a good sign.

His father was sitting up against a stack of pillows, the *London Times* folded on the blanket beside him. The color on his face was much improved, but whether from recovering health or from a great deal of ire at his interfering heir was unclear. Either one was a good sign.

"Good evening, sir. You are looking in much better curl."

"No thanks to you." The old man's eyes blazed as they locked on his son. "What is this nonsense about building a new fence along the Wells road? And putting new roofs on *all* the tenant cottages. Why, that will cost a king's ransom."

Drew resisted the urge to smile. Despite what his father had declared, he still cared about the estate and its expenses. "The fence, sir, has tumbled down in five or six places. Over ten sheep were lost the last year before Clifton disposed of the herd for you. It's in the ledgers. As to the cottages, they are unfit to let until they have been refurbished and all but two are vacant. We mustn't allow all that fallow ground to go unfarmed, sir. It's the lifeblood of the estate."

A slender hand plucked at the covers a moment, then the baron grunted. "And you've funds enough to make these changes without borrowing the ready?"

"I do, sir."

Lord Rowland settled back into his pillows. His face held a hint of pride at his son's accomplishment. "Tell me about your life since you went away."

Drew pulled a straight-backed chair to the side of the bed and settled himself. He spoke for some thirty minutes, neither sugar-coating the hard times nor inflating the successes. He merely told a tale. At last, he got to the point where he had been pressed in London and rescued by Jack, then to his return home.

The old gentleman sat in silence for a moment, then said, "I'm not saying it wasn't hard, Andrew, but if I'd had half as much luck as you, I'd not be in my current straitened circumstances."

Drew stared at his father a long time. It suddenly dawned on him that the baron was one of those men who thought life depended on luck and not on hard work and initiative. His belief in luck was perhaps the thing that made him a hardened gamester. Work was for others, not for titled gentlemen. Drew had learned long ago that one wasn't likely to change a man's philosophy or beliefs. Very often only time and learning from one's mistakes firsthand could do that, and even then not always, as his father had proven. Lord Rowland believed in luck and would likely continue to game until his dying day. He couldn't change that part of his father. He could only help him regain his health, hopefully.

An idea flashed in Drew's head. "Father, there is something I would discuss with you."

Rowland's brows grew flat. "A bit late to be asking my opinion on anything. What do you want to know?"

"I have discovered the location of Miss Blanchett, and—"

The old gentleman sat up, there was a spark of interest in his eyes. "The sickly child is alive?"

"*Miss Blanchett* is alive and she is nether sickly nor a child, sir. The problem is that her circumstances are not good. Yet, I'm not fool enough to return her home and think she'd be safe." Drew watched his father's face. There was no guilt there; only excitement that the terms of the betrothal might at last be fulfilled and the monies paid. It was rather disillusioning to find that his father wasn't a better man. At least it enforced his belief the gentleman hadn't been involved in the plot to murder Jacinda's father.

Lord Rowland reached out and grabbed his son's

hand in a surprising strong grip. "You must marry the chit at once, Andrew."

Drew's heart plummeted. When he'd first determined to come back, deep inside, he'd hoped he wouldn't be forced to fulfill the terms of the betrothal agreement. The document the solicitor had shown him stated that if Miss Blanchett wished she could refuse the marriage. Then his mind settled on the hazel eyes that had stared up at him at the glen, of the full, kissable mouth and the firm breasts outlined by the muslin wrap while she'd stood in the pool with the water cascading off her porcelain skin. Something stirred in him. Great heavens, he'd known she was a woman for barely two hours and already he was lusting after her. Would such a marriage be so bad? He might not love her but at least he admired her spirit. He was glad she was no longer the frail child he remembered, for this Miss Blanchett stirred his blood.

He sat up straighter in the chair when a second truth dawned on him. He didn't know if there was someone else in Jacinda's life, but he had the impression not. There was certainly no one in his, nor had been since Mariah. But his father had the right idea. If Drew married Jacinda, he would become her heir and there would no longer be a reason for her to die. She would no longer be in danger. Not to mention, it might help assuage some of his guilt. He still had a sense that his father and Blanchett might have triggered the murder with the proposed marriage.

Drew nodded at his father. He knew their reasons for the wedding to take place at once weren't the same, but that didn't matter. "I shall wed her as soon as a license can be procured."

CHAPTER FIVE

The following day dawned bright and sunny over Somerset. Drew rose early, hoping to catch Jacinda before she started her chores to tell her what decision he'd made about her. As he strolled though the gardens he wondered what she would look like fashionably dressed with her hair properly done. The face was too delicate for a boy, but would it be pretty as a woman? He was surprised at how anxious he was to see her properly attired. But no matter how she looked, he fully intended to do his duty.

He scanned the gardens but there was no sign of her at work. He made his way to the small cottage in the woods. There he discovered Ben lacing his boots on the front bench.

"Good morning, lad, where is Miss Blanchett?"

There was little welcome in Ben young face. He angrily scanned the area to make certain they were alone. "Don't call her that, sir. Someone might hear."

"Very well, where is Jack?" Drew settled on the bench beside the boy.

"Gone to have Seth sharpen the scythes for the lads coming on Monday." Ben went back to tying his brogans, ignoring the captain.

Drew understood that in the boy's mind he'd suddenly

gone from benefactor to dangerous meddler, so he set about trying to mend the relationship. "Ben, I'm still your friend and as such I want to help. You know Jack shouldn't be here working as my gardener. She's a gently bred female."

The boy jumped to his feet, facing Drew. "You're not going to send her back over there with someone wanting to do her in, are you? Besides, she can take care of herself. She's not one of those namby-pamby misses that has to be sheltered from everything."

"I know she has weathered her life on the run better than most would, but don't you think she deserves what is rightfully hers? To live at Chettwood, go to parties, and have a normal life. I have a plan that will take her out of harm's way."

The boy was scarcely more than a child, but more mature than most of his age. "She does deserve to go home. What have you in mind?"

Drew was struck by how Jacinda's influence had bettered young Ben. If what Drew suspected was true, he was a highwayman's son. Yet, the lad could read and speak as if he had grown up in one of the large houses in this neighborhood. He wouldn't fully understand how much she'd done for him until he was grown. For the lad, it wasn't about her fortune—he loved her for herself.

"You know that Miss, er—that the lady and I are betrothed. It was arranged by our fathers years ago. I'm convinced that was what brought about Blanchett's death and the danger to Jacinda. Someone wants her fortune before she can wed and have a family."

"Aye, Aunt Trudy always said as much."

"Well, if I marry her, then by law what is hers becomes mine and there is no reason for anyone to murder her."

The lad stared out at the trees a moment, then faced

Drew with troubled eyes. "But she still loses her fortune in that plan."

Drew shook his head. "It's not like that, lad. I'll have her solicitor make arrangements for her to keep control of everything that's hers. No one need know."

Ben searched the captain's face a moment as if he could find evidence of the truth there. "You'll let her keep what's hers?"

Drew nodded.

"It's a sound plan, Captain, but there's one problem."

"If you think I would harm her, lad—"

"That's not the problem, sir. I've acquitted you of being involved in anything bad to do with this. It's only that Jack is pretty stubborn. If she gets it in her head she doesn't want to marry you there's nothing you or I or even the likes of the Prince of Wales could do to change her mind."

Such romantic nonsense might prove to be a problem. Drew had been so busy planning her future he'd given little thought to *her* wishes. "Has she taken me in aversion?" Somehow he didn't want to think he'd done anything that offended her. As Jack he'd liked her drive and determination, so surely he'd admire her as a female.

"Oh, nothing like that. It's only she's female and they have the oddest notions about love and marriage. I heard her tell Lili that one would be a fool to marry without loving one's partner."

If the boy was right, Drew would have to handle matters carefully. Without careful handling, he would frighten her into running away and if he'd learned anything about Jack, it was that she was fully capable of doing just that. But what could he do? If only there were someone to encourage her to do as he asked.

Someone whom she trusted . . . Then it dawned on him. Who was the one person she'd kept informed of her well-being these eight years past? Her father's solicitor, Thomas Wilkins. That was the one person whose support Drew must enlist.

He promised Ben he'd come up with a solution and the boy headed out towards the stables, leaving Drew on the bench to ponder how he would handle Jacinda. He had to get her to agree to return to London. His mind was so busy with plans that it was several minutes before he realized he was no longer alone.

A footfall brought him from his thoughts. Drew looked up to see Jacinda standing in the clearing in front of him, the scythes over her shoulder. He rose and bowed. She hesitated a moment, then greeted him as she lowered the tools to the ground. "Is there a problem, Captain?"

"No, but I told you I needed to think about what best to do about your situation. I'm still uncomfortable about your position here." She began to protest, but he held up his hand. "Please hear me out. I think we should return to London and speak with your father's solicitor."

Jacinda frowned. "Why?"

"There are several reasons. First and foremost is that he has been the one investigating your father's death. He would know best where we should focus our attention. It would be fruitless to waste weeks asking questions about someone who has already been proven to be innocent. Also, I think it important that you establish your claim before you are one-and-twenty. It seems some of your relatives want you declared dead." It bothered Drew that Mrs. Devere had offhandedly suggested such at tea, urging him not to have false hope. She'd even gone so far as to remind him that he was now wealthy and didn't need to dangle after an heiress.

Drew watched the uncertainty play on Jacinda's face. He didn't want to give her the other reason he wanted to see Wilkins. He needed the solicitor's support before he informed the lady of his intentions. At last, she seemed to come to some decision.

"I do think I should speak with Mr. Wilkins. I should like to make arrangements for Ben to have a separate income in case something were to happen—"

Drew's hand closed over her shoulder. "I won't let anything happen. I promise."

Their eyes locked and Drew once again marveled at the length of her lashes. How had he not seen that "Jack" was a woman? Because he'd been too taken up with his own problems.

She broke into his musing when she asked, "When will we depart?"

Relief washed over Drew and his hand dropped from her. "I shall be interviewing bailiffs today, and tomorrow is Sunday. Why not leave after the workers arrive on Monday? That way you can instruct them as to what still needs to be done. There is plenty to keep them busy. Hopefully we shall return by Friday at the latest."

"Very well, and may Ben go with us?"

"He is most welcome." With the boy in London, Drew would have one more voice supporting the plan for them to wed.

"Miss Blanchett and Captain Andrew Morrow to see you, sir!"

Thomas Wilkins blinked his eyes twice as his clerk's words sank into his busy brain. The summer heat in the

upstairs office had left his face damp and pink but the
news just imparted made his cheeks flush red. He looked
closely at his clerk thinking perhaps his young employee
had taken to tippling at his desk. "I am not amused, Harwick. No one has seen either one of those poor children
in eight years. If you have taken to drink . . ."

Harwick swallowed hard. His employer was not a
cruel man, but he certainly had little sense of humor and
if the pair in the front office were playing a prank, it
would be his post. "I swear, sir, I've not had a drop. The
gentleman gave me his card, albeit his companion don't
look like a Miss Blanchett to me, but a lad." A trembling
hand came out and dropped the rectangular cream vel-
lum on the solicitor's desk.

Mr. Wilkins snatched it up and pushed his glasses up
on his nose, the better to see the plain lettering. Could
it possibly be true? Excitement coursed through his
veins. Could his search for the child be at an end? He
stood and gestured at Harwick even as he reached for
his jacket that hung on the back of his chair. "Show
them in at once, man."

Within minutes a tall, neatly dressed gentleman and
what appeared to be a young lad of fifteen or sixteen
stepped into the large office. Wilkins gaze roved over
the lad's heart-shaped face. He scarcely recognized
young Jacinda. If not for the tiny mole at the corner of
her mouth, he would not have known her, for in most
other ways she was much changed. His strongest memories were of a delicate little girl who used to come in
and beg her father to override Cousin Millie's orders to
stay indoors. Gone was the plain child who was so fragile that a puff of wind would have knocked her over. In
her stead was a young woman with an attractive face,
and maturity and confidence in her hazel eyes. He sus-

pected a hint of stubbornness, as well, for this was no bashful miss as she met his gaze squarely. His only complaint was that she was dressed as a boy instead of as the proper lady she'd been raised.

He scarcely paid attention to the young gentleman since he'd never met the baron's son. The solicitor hurried from behind the desk to take the young lady's hand. "Miss Blanchett, welcome. And may I say you are looking fit."

Jacinda extended her hand to the gentleman who was a bit grayer and perhaps a bit heavier but still had the bluest eyes she'd ever seen. "Mr. Wilkins, how are you?"

"Much better now that I see you with my own eyes and know that you are well and safe." The solicitor put out his hand to Captain Morrow. "I'm not certain how the two of you came to be together, but you, sir, seem to have made good use of the years, Captain, is it? Do sit down and tell me all, both of you."

Jacinda and Drew sat in the seats to which the old gentleman gestured. Jacinda waited until he'd gone back behind the desk and settled himself. He offered them tea but both declined.

"I'm all ears, child. Your letters told me only that you were safe. Where have you been all this time?"

It took some twenty minutes for her to tell her story. Mr. Wilkins didn't say a word, but when she told him of Trudy's death, he made a noise of sympathy and shook his head. When she got to the part about meeting Captain Morrow, that gentleman took over and briefly explained he'd only learned about Mr. Blanchett's death on his return from India. He told of his unfortunate encounter with the Press Gang and being rescued by "Jack" and Ben Trudeau. Lastly, he told of discovering

Jacinda's true identity only after he'd hired her to work as gardener at his father's estate in Somerset.

Astonished, Wilkins face turned a bit ashen. "Miss Jacinda, have you already been home?"

"I have been to the captain's home. Do not think that my relatives have learned of my whereabouts, for I assure you they have not."

The solicitor slumped back in his chair in silence for a moment. "You've both had your own adventures. Unfortunately, despite Bow Street's best efforts we still don't know who killed your father. And you are certain they tried to harm you?"

"They searched the rocks for me and left only when a carriage could be heard coming."

The old gentleman's brows moved lower. "Well, then, my dear, you could be in as grave a danger today as you were eight years ago."

"Mr. Wilkins," Captain Morrow asked, "who would inherit after Miss Blanchett died?"

"That is what has me puzzled, Captain. I wrote the codicil to Blanchett's will when Jacinda was five. Besides her, there is no heir at present." On seeing the puzzled looks on his visitors faces, he continued. "Your father arranged that if for any reason you should die without issue before you reached your majority or before you marry, his funds and estate should be held in trust for the offspring of his brother Matthew's children. Mr. Claude Blanchett, who is unmarried, and his sister, Mrs. Jane Iverson, who is two years married, are both childless."

Drew Morrow rose and went to stand behind Jacinda. "Then perhaps there was some other reason for the attempt on her life."

The solicitor pressed his lips primly together a moment

and his face flushed. "This is a rather difficult matter to discuss, my dear. Your father was . . ." he hesitated.

"My father was a philanderer." She said it, but it was difficult for her to fathom. She had loved him dearly but it was only after she was older that she understood the hurt he had inflicted on her mother.

The old gentleman nodded his head. "He adored women from his earliest years, but I cannot think that had anything to do with his death. He was always very discreet. No, I'm certain it's the fortune. What else could it be? Why else involve you if not for the fortune?"

The captain leaned forward. "Are there any suspects?"

The solicitor shrugged. "If I were a betting man, I would say either Matthew Blanchett's son, Claude, or Giles Devere."

"My cousins?"

"Both have expensive tastes, both could use a fortune for different reasons, and both have shown some interest in finding you, my dear. Albeit they might have inquired for the information on their parents' behalf."

Jacinda wasn't close with either cousin, but still it was hard for her to believe that Giles or Claude would have hired someone to kill her and her father. Yet money made men do dreadful things. During her time on London's streets, she'd seen men fight over a shilling. "How would they benefit if they aren't in my father's will?'

Wilkins arched a brow at her." I've given it a great deal of thought and I suspect that over the last few days of your father's life he may have drawn up a new will. I've even convinced your Cousin Millicent to search for one, but she's had no success so far."

"Is that very likely?" Jacinda remembered that something had been troubling her father those last few days.

He'd had numerous visitors but had explained none of it to them.

"It's possible if he were in a hurry, he drafted a will on his own, using his old will as a model. It is distinctly possible the will is somewhere in Chettwood Manor and may tell us who would benefit if you . . ." The old gentleman's face flushed crimson.

"Were dead." Jacinda finished the sentence for the old gentleman. "Then I must return home. I must look for that will."

"My dear child, that would only be safe if you were married." The old solicitors' eyes widened as his own words struck him. He looked to her companion. "Captain, are you willing to marry Miss Blanchett as the terms of the betrothal contact state?"

"I am. 'Tis an excellent solution, sir."

Startled, Jacinda turned to the captain. His charmingly innocent grin didn't fool her for a moment. She'd been duped into coming to London. There he sat, looking like the cat who'd eaten the canary, and a very handsome one at that, his smile making him too charming for her to be truly angry.

A strange sensation raced through her at the thought of marrying the gentleman. It would be wonderful to allow someone else to be the strong one for a change. For the past five years, since Trudy had fallen ill, Jacinda had managed every aspect of her life and Ben's. Her gaze played over Captain Morrow's strong face and she sensed that he would protect her in all things.

Then her mother's words echoed in her mind: *He must love you as you love him.* She wasn't even certain about her own feelings . . . how could she know his? He was a man one could admire, but she wasn't completely certain she could trust him, so how could she think about love?

"Miss Blanchett," the captain sat forward in the seat beside her, breaking into her chaotic thoughts. "Jacinda, we have been betrothed these eight years. The papers were duly signed. I read them recently at my father's solicitor's office. I made a mistake that day so long ago but I have returned, and I intend to fulfill—"

Jacinda held up her hand to stop his words as she shook her head. It was evident what he intended to say and she didn't want to hear the words. He was going to talk about their duty to their fathers. Why, he hadn't even bothered to take her hand as he was proposing to her. "No!"

"My dear, Miss Blanchett," the solicitor's calm voice interrupted. "You mustn't be missish. We are talking about your life. The captain is willing; I cannot see any reason to delay. It is a very good match, especially since the captain is no longer deficient in funds."

Jacinda's thoughts were in a swirl. They were talking of funds, not love. Marriage was too important for her to tie herself to a man who would marry her out of duty. Still she knew her life to be in danger, and these two men would never allow her back into Chettwood without the protection of a husband.

"Jacinda," the captain spoke her name softly and the intimacy of it sent a strange tingle through her. "I shall have Mr. Wilkins draw up a settlement that will allow you to keep your fortune separate."

She stared into the depths of his dark green eyes and found herself wanting to say yes. He was handsome, smart, and kind, what more could she want in a husband? But the same thing kept repeating in her head. *Love,* she wanted love.

"Child, a husband could save your life, and—"

Suddenly, Jacinda knew what to do. "I agree, Mr. Wilkins. A husband is what I need. Captain Morrow and I shall *pretend* to be married, if you are still willing to do this my way, sir." Seeing the protest on his well-shaped lips, she crossed her arms. "We pretend to be married, or I go back to pulling weeds in your garden, Captain."

The two gentlemen exchanged an exasperated glance about the obstinacy of females, but at last the captain nodded his assent. "Very well, I shall do it your way. But you must promise you will be careful."

"I have no wish to depart this world, Captain. I shall be very careful."

His gaze raked her. "And of course, you cannot continue to dress as a lad."

Jacinda tugged at her waistcoat. She hadn't even thought about her clothes. "New gowns?" A thrill of delight stirred in her. She'd never really had an opportunity to choose her own clothes. Aunt Devere and Cousin Millie had always done that when she was a youngster and there had been no pretty gowns while she'd been in hiding. Then she was suddenly guilty. This wasn't about how she would look, but finding her father's killer.

The old solicitor rose. "My dear, allow me to take you to my daughter. No doubt her *modeste* would be delighted to serve you. With your funds we shall have you turned out as a proper lady by the end of the week."

"Here are the marriage lines I had Harwick draw up for you." Mr. Wilkins handed the paper across the desk to Drew some ten days later. "They won't stand for too close a scrutiny, so do be careful. We chose the parish in Tunbridge Wells in County Kent. A fair distance from London and especially Westbury. We didn't want one of her relations going through the registry for there would be no evidence of a wedding."

Drew scanned the document. It looked official enough to him but then he couldn't say he'd ever seen marriage lines before.

Mr. Wilkins continued. "Also, if you will, give this document to Miss Blanchett."

"Perhaps you should begin to refer to her as Mrs. Morrow." Drew smiled at the old gentleman as he folded the phony license and put it in his pocket.

The solicitor nodded and continued, "I have set aside twenty thousand pounds into a separate account for young Ben Trudeau and purchased a small business for a Miss Lili LeBeau of Wapping as Miss Blanchett requested. Even should, God forbid, something happen to her, no one could touch that money or the business. For the lad, the money is duly his to do with as he will on reaching one-and-twenty. I have made you and Miss, er, I mean Mrs. Morrow joint on the lad's guardianship."

"Nothing will happen to Jacinda, sir. I promise." Perhaps he was being overly confident, but he wouldn't allow anyone to inflict more harm on her.

Mr. Wilkins sat back in his chair. Worried lights hovered in the depths of his eyes. "When do you leave for Somerset? I have written to her family and informed them that she is found and returning home within the next week."

"The carriage I hired is being loaded even as we speak. Your daughter is dropping her at the hotel this afternoon." Drew was anxious to see her. It had taken the better part of a week but there were three trunks already loaded with Jacinda's new wardrobe, as well as the new clothing for young Ben. They'd scarcely seen Jacinda all week, what with fittings and shopping. "We shall go straight to Chettwood Manor. I have so many workmen at Rowland Park making repairs I thought to use that as an excuse for our staying at her home."

There could be little doubt that was where they should be, but there was also the increased danger. "Do be careful, sir."

"You forget that Ben will be helping me. Together we shall keep her safe." Drew rose.

"I wasn't referring to Mrs. Morrow, but to you, Captain. By marrying Miss Blanchett, you have put yourself in harm's way if our murderer is quite determined."

"That was the plan, Mr. Wilkins. Better me than a defenseless woman." On those words, Drew departed.

A knock sounded at the door of the hotel room and before Jacinda could say a word, Ben's head appeared round the door. "May I come in?"

"Of course." She turned from the looking glass, where she had been admiring Madame Chloe's handiwork since Mrs. Houston had left her to return to family. Even now, Jacinda was stunned by the attractive young female in the glass. For the first time in eight years she felt like Miss Blanchett of Chettwood Manor.

Ben stepped in from the hallway and Jacinda hardly recognized him. The captain had had the lad's hair cut fashionably short and provided him with a new wardrobe. He looked quite the young gentleman despite the fact his mother was a chambermaid and his father a highwayman. It went a long way to convincing Jacinda that much could be done to improve the plight of the common man. Perhaps if so many youngsters weren't out on the streets fending for themselves at an early age, there would be less crime. Once she was back at Chettwood and established she must look into founding an orphanage that would teach children and not just warehouse them.

The lad eyed her expectantly for a moment and when she remained mute because she was lost in thought, he said, "Jack, am I not as fine as five pence?" She smiled as he turned around slowly for her to admire all his finery.

Jacinda smiled at his continued use of the old name and at his pride in his new looks. She couldn't have been prouder of him if he truly were her own little brother. But she was certain he wouldn't want any untoward display of affection so she merely said, "You are even finer than that. You will have all the young ladies in Westbury after you."

The lad grunted, but whether from pleasure or disgust was unclear. His eyes suddenly widened as he took in Jacinda's new apparel. "Bloody hell, if you ain't beautiful, Jack."

Jacinda was pleased at his compliment, but not his words. "What have I told you about such language young man? A gentleman never says such and I do so dislike the word 'ain't.'"

Ben straightened, folded his hands politely in front of him and in a deep voice said, "My dear Miss Blanchett, you are quite exquisite, if I may say." Then he bowed with a great flourish and twinkling eyes. "How was that?"

They both fell into peals of laughter, which they had a difficult time controlling even after a knock sounded on the door. Before Jacinda could say a word, Ben opened the door to reveal Captain Morrow.

Her heart seemed to skip a beat at the sight of him. He

looked handsome in his blue jacket, blue and white stripped waistcoat, and tan breeches with Hessians. She'd seen little of Ben and the captain; Mrs. Houston had insisted that she stay at Half Moon Street with her since she had no maid to keep things proper. But her week had been quite fun, shopping, playing with her hostess's young girls, and getting back into the feel of being a lady.

The captain stood for a moment in the doorway. He couldn't quite fathom that the beauty before him was once young Jack. Her golden brown hair had been styled into fashionable curls with a ribbon run though them. She looked elegant in a pale green traveling gown that showed her slender figure to perfection. The gown was trimmed with gold military-style frogging at the bodice, a ruff of gold lace inset at her collar. Tiny black leaves had been embroidered along the hem and at the ends of her sleeves. A straw casquet bonnet with small green flowers along the brim lay on the table beside her

He took her hand and pressed a kiss on her glove. "My dear, you are too lovely for words." Was that a look of fear in her hazel eyes, or merely uncertainty for what lay ahead? If the boy hadn't been there, the urge to take her in his arms would have been too great. Drew released her hand and stepped back.

"Yeah," Ben said, "who would have thought Jack could look a proper lady?"

Both adults stared at him as if he'd spoken a curse word in polite company. "Uh, you know what I meant." When neither one agreed, he added, "Perhaps we should be going, Jack. It's a long ride back to Somerset."

The captain offered Jacinda his arm. "The lad is right on that account. We want to reach Chettwood in a timely manner."

A slight tremor went through her arm as she lifted it

to take his. His hand closed over her smaller one, which rested on his sleeve. "Don't be frightened, my dear. I promise I'll protect you."

She gave him such a trusting smile, he felt he couldn't fail. He would protect her at all cost.

The sun had disappeared behind the trees as their carriage turned into the long drive of Chettwood Manor. Jacinda fidgeted with the strings to her green reticule as the familiar grounds passed the windows. She spied the family of ducks she'd adored as a young child and was delighted to discover they still resided on the ornamental pond, or at least their descendants did. Several mother ducks, their young in tow, glided to the far side of the lake as the carriage drove along the gravel drive. A memory of her cousin Claude pushing her down the steps of the gazebo near the water flashed in her mind. His sister, Jane, had kicked him in the shin for doing it. She wondered who among her relatives would be at the manor.

As they passed the open meadow, she recalled how Ben's grandfather had taught her to ride. Her mother and Cousin Millie had looked on as if the gentle Snowflake were some dangerous stallion instead of an old Shetland pony. There were so many memories, good and bad, proving she still had a strong connection to this place.

The manor came into view and a strange twinge occurred in her stomach. She was coming home at last. Jacinda stared at the huge building, knowing that things were going to be quite different. Her father was no longer there to see to everything. She would not only be the mistress of the manor but responsible for the entire estate by year's end.

The carriage circled the flagstone courtyard and drew to a halt under a large portico. To Jacinda's surprise, the oversized oak doors opened in an instant, as if every one had been waiting behind it for days. Stritch and what seemed a bevy of servants spilled onto the front stairs, the great hall chandelier lit and casting an inviting glow behind them. They beamed at her as if each and every one had received a raise in salary that very morning.

Jacinda stomach churned as she caught sight of the interior of her home. At first she thought she might be sickening, then she realized what she was feeling wasn't illness, but fear. She shrank back into the squabs, wishing she didn't have to face all these people—servants and family alike. Someone here wished to do her harm. Not only that, they expected her to know what to do: how to run a house, how to run an estate, how to be the lady. This was like nothing she'd ever done.

A hand closed over her gloved fists, which lay clenched on her lap. She looked up into Captain Morrow's kind eyes.

"Where is that fearless young Jack who faced down the King's Impressment service?"

Her gaze darted to the waiting servants, then back to the gentleman. "I think I might have left him in Madame Chloe's changing rooms along with his coat and breeches."

The gentleman chuckled. "I think not. What made Jack strong is still inside Miss Jacinda Blanchett."

Jacinda wasn't so sure. Jack's life had been more about the basics of survival: food, shelter, and taking care of Ben. Here she was rather like a boat without a rudder, adrift and uncertain what direction to take with people who'd become strangers. Then the gentleman squeezed her hand and she suddenly realized she had her very own captain to help her navigate these dangerous waters. She gave him as brave a smile as she could muster.

The door to the carriage opened and the butler, whose tone was as staid as usual but whose eyes were alive with delight, said, "Welcome back to Chettwood, Miss Jacinda."

She stiffened her spine and allowed the old servant to take her hand and help her down the steps. Ben had already scrambled down from the driver's perch where he'd begged to ride after their last stop. In truth, she suspected he'd taken exception to the information that she'd taken Mr. Wilkins's advice and decided to send him to school. At present, he was surprisingly subdued in front of the staff.

"Stritch, 'tis good to see you looking so well and fit." As the captain joined her, she gestured at him. "I hope you will welcome my husband, Captain Andrew Morrow."

The old servant did an excellent job of maintaining his composure but there was a soft titter of interest from the maids and footmen that one raised brow from Stritch ended. He bowed formally. "May I wish you happy, madam. And you, sir, are most welcome at Chettwood."

"And this" Jacinda said, "is Ben Trudeau, Trudy's nephew. He will be staying here in the house until he goes away to school in the fall." Watching the servants' appalled expressions, her tone took on a hint of steel. "He has been my family for the past eight years and I expect him to be treated as such."

To her surprise, Ben drew his hands behind him just

the way the captain had and bowed. "I am delighted to be here, Stritch. Miss Blanchett has told us this is the best run house in the neighborhood."

The old butler didn't say a word, but Jacinda sensed that Ben had taken just the right deferent tone with the servant.

"Jacinda?" Cousin Millie interrupted the meeting when she appeared in the doorway and stared at the visitors with nervous anticipation.

Eight years had taken a toll on the older woman. Her hair was more gray than brown now. Lines radiated from her eyes and mouth. Hollows had permanently settled in her cheeks, but still there was joy in her eyes.

"Cousin Millie, it's good to be home at last." Jacinda hurried up the stairs and hugged the woman, who seemed to be more frail than she remembered, but, then, perhaps it was only that she herself had grown strong.

Millicent placed her hands round her niece's face and seemed to drink in her countenance. "Child, you look so much like your mother it makes me want to weep. I have worried so about you and here you are all grown and . . ." she looked past Jacinda at the captain, "according to Mr. Wilkins's most recent letter, married."

Drew appeared at Jacinda's side and introductions were made. Millicent frowned at him. "Well, young man, I hope your have outgrown that wild streak that we all remember."

"Cousin," Jacinda chided. "He is *Captain* Morrow, not some schoolboy." He was going to a great deal of trouble to help her, not to mention the danger he'd placed himself in. She certainly didn't want her family treating him badly.

But the captain took the jibe in stride. "Just the indiscretions of an idle youth, Miss Markham, I promise you."

The lady harrumphed as if to say only time would tell. Without another word to him, she slid her arm through her niece's. "Do you wish to go to your rooms and refresh yourselves first or meet the rest of the family?"

Jacinda removed her bonnet and gloves, handing them to a nearby footman as the captain surrendered his hat to Stritch. "That won't be necessary. We stopped in Wells and had supper. Let us not keep the others waiting."

"Come, my dear, they are in the Gold Drawing Room. We've had word from your uncle that business at present keeps him in town, but he asks that you write and tell him if there is anything you need. Claude is away on business and Jane sends you her best but she won't come until the autumn for she is much involved with her charity with the Widow and Orphans Fund, and thinks as well that you might need time to readjust to life at the manor." Millie escorted her down the hall.

The room was much as Jacinda remembered it, but she'd seen little of the formal rooms, having been considered still in the nursery. Her Aunt Devere and cousins were huddled together near an open window, the growing darkness still warm from the day's heat. There was a moment's hesitation as the newly arrived party entered the room, as if each group was measuring the other.

At last Mrs. Devere hurried forward, Giles and Prudence in her wake. "Well, Jacinda, you cannot know how we have all worried about you. Have we not Giles? Prudence?" The pair murmured their agreement.

Giles smirked and simpered. "Cousin Jacinda, welcome home." He looked her over as if inspecting a horse, then he laughed, "Why, cousin, if I'd known you would grow up to be such a beauty I would have been kinder."

A cool smile touched Jacinda's lips. His new toadying was even less desirable than his old needling of her. Deciding that she must make the best of the situation at present, she merely turned to her companion. "May I present my husband, Captain Morrow."

Prudence's lips puckered in disappointment. "Captain, you didn't tell us that you were intending to marry our cousin out of hand as soon as she was found. One would think you in need of her fortune."

The captain smiled politely, despite the lady's tone. "One might think that if one didn't know better. But, my dear Mrs. Tyne, who could think of fortunes after taking one look at my wife's beautiful face. I've come to believe there truly is a thing such as love at first sight."

He gave Jacinda such a look that she suddenly wished his words were true. Her cheeks warmed and she was relieved when her Cousin Millie suggested they all sit down and she would order tea.

"But who is this adorable child?" Mrs. Devere's words were in direct contrast with the look she cast at Ben.

"Forgive me for forgetting about this scamp, but he is not usually so quiet." Jacinda slid her around arm Ben's shoulders to leave her relations in no doubt that she held the lad in great affection. She made the introduction.

Startled looks settled over all their faces. Cousin Millie frowned. "But was not Trudy's brother a . . .well, that is . . ."

Prudence's tone was amused. "Highwayman is the word, madam."

Anger fueled Jacinda's courage. She had to be strong

and not just for herself. "Cousin, if you wish to remain a member of this household, I wish never to hear such again. Ben is my ward and shall be treated as such by all who reside here. He has been as a brother to me since I was thirteen and so he shall always remain." She smiled down at him and he up at her. Only a blind person would be in doubt of the affection between them.

Mrs. Tyne's cheeks flamed red and she eyed her newly rediscovered cousin with a measuring gaze. "I—I meant no disrespect, Jacinda." Seeing that her words had little effect, she stepped forward and kissed Ben's cheek. "Welcome to Chettwood. Would you like to go riding with Giles and me in the morning?"

Ben looked from the lady to Jacinda and back. "Thank you, but I fear I cannot properly ride a horse as yet. The captain here has promised to teach me." He grinned, willing to take the lady at face value.

Jacinda would give him a warning in the morning. But, then, perhaps her cousins had changed. She knew from what Martha had told her that day in the woods that they both had known difficult times. One mustn't be so quick to judge.

"I should be delighted to ride with you once the captain deems you safe to leave the paddock." Prudence stepped back beside her mother.

There was an uncomfortable silence for a moment, then Cousin Millie took Jacinda's arm and led her to the sitting area. "Prudence, ring for tea. I'm certain we should all like to hear about all that has befallen Jacinda since we last saw her."

The evening finished with Cook's best efforts to impress as well as an exchange of information. They learned of Jacinda's eight years missing and over the course of the evening she learned that Cousin Millie had

run the estate with Weems's able help. Prudence had
fallen in love and married a young adventurer who'd
gotten himself killed in a duel over cards, leaving her
penniless and forced to return to Chettwood. As for
Giles, he lived the life of a country gentleman on his allowance, always on the hunt for a wife with fortune and
position, always short of funds, and always falling
below his mother's expectations. Mrs. Devere's sole
purpose in life still revolved around protecting and pro-
moting her children. So, all three were still dependent
on Blanchett generosity. As far as Jacinda could tell, it
seemed that little had changed since she'd gone away.

CHAPTER SIX

A long clock in the hall chimed the hour of midnight. Jacinda listened to the lonely sound as she stood in her night rail and wrapper. The large apartment where she stood had formerly been her mother's. She'd dismissed Martha only moments before, exhausted from the long evening with her relatives.

Still, she found herself reluctant to retire. Perhaps it was because this room was so full of memories of her mother. Often Jacinda would come early and find the lady still in her bedclothes, writing to friends and relatives or waiting for her only child so she could simply play with Jacinda before her busy morning began. It was a large, well-furnished room with delicate rosewood furniture that her mother had brought with her from her own home. Watered silk paper on the walls with tiny pink roses had been personally chosen by the lady.

Jacinda ran her hand over her mother's favorite inlaid secretary and there was a part of her that felt the lady's presence—a decided calm came over her. For the first time, she felt as if her dear mother were watching over her. It made her feel safe, if not elsewhere at Chettwood then at least here in this room.

A knock sounded and for a moment Jacinda was

confused as to where it came from. Then she realized
it was at the communicating door between her room
and the captain's. In his masquerade as her husband,
he was given her father's old rooms. She called for
him to enter and he stepped through the door. His gaze
swept her from head to toe, an appreciative gleam in
his eyes. She wore only her nightwear. How could she
have been so foolish to invite him in? What must he
think of her? She pulled her wrapper tighter. It was
rather a useless effort, for it was a pretty frilly garment, so sheer her night rail was visible through the
diaphanous muslin. Mrs. Houston had picked it out,
declaring that it was quite the thing.

Jacinda noted he, too, was dressed to retire . . . or perhaps she should say undress, as her gaze went to the
deep vee of his green brocade banyan. A strange knot
formed in her stomach at the sight of bare skin and a
tuft of dark hair on his tanned chest. She forced her gaze
away, then, thinking herself a coward, looked back to his
face. A twinkle lurked in his emerald eyes at her nervous reaction to him.

"You do look ravishing, my dear, and I am sorely
tempted, but I have merely come to inform you that
Miss Markham wishes to see me in the library at nine
to turn over the ledgers and accounts. I thought you
might prefer to be present since you shall be the one
who will in truth be manager here."

She bit at her lip a moment, not realizing how enticing such a gesture looked to the captain. "I haven't a
clue how to go about managing an estate, sir. Whatever
shall I do?"

He was slow to answer. At last he pulled his attention
from her mouth. "It's simply a matter of common sense,
Jacinda. Besides, you will do fine once all is explained.

After all, your cousin appears to have done an excellent job of managing things with little experience. Weems has demonstrated himself a very capable steward."

"Yes, he has guided my cousin well."

"If you have any questions, don't hesitate to ask me. While I'm more familiar with sails and currents, I, too, have been mastering how to manage an estate and will gladly share what I've learned. I'm certain you shall manage things quite well." He stood in silence, staring at her as if he would memorize every detail.

Her heart pounded strongly in her chest. "W-was there something else?"

"Something else?" He straightened and cleared his throat. "Um, yes, I want you to promise me you won't go anywhere outside the manor alone." Noting her frown, he took a step closer and his masculine scent tickled her senses. "I promised to protect you, but I cannot always be in your company or the others will grow suspicious. Make certain you are with someone during the day and especially if you must be outdoors. That is where you are most vulnerable."

"Vulnerable!" The word and all it insinuated pricked Jacinda's vanity. Had she not proven herself capable of handling her own affairs? "Sir, I will have you know that I have taken care of myself for the better part of eight years." Her cheeks warmed with indignation. She hated that he thought her so weak. She was no fool; she knew there was danger here.

He ran a hand through his hair, tousling the short curls. "Perhaps vulnerable was a poor choice of words. Easier prey. It's not such a difficult thing I ask. Simply stay inside unless you are with someone. There is safety in numbers."

"I won't be a prisoner in the manor." She glared up at

him. "I have lived in the worst parts of London. I do assure you I can take care of myself. Besides I shall never learn anything if I hide away in my room."

His green eyes darkened and he grasped her shoulders. "It's not safe; I won't risk—"

She thrust a hand on his chest to force him to see she was her own master. The brocade fabric felt warm, the body hard and muscular beneath. She drew back as if she'd been stung. Suddenly the argument didn't seem important. "I—I will always take one of the footmen or grooms with me if I do decide to venture out."

For a moment they became like two animals sparring for dominance. Their eyes locked and a strange quiet blanketed them. Jacinda's heart raced as the captain's gaze dropped to her lips. She thought he would kiss her. Anticipation surged through her. To her surprised disappointment, he released her and stepped back.

"Never go without an *armed* footman or groom."

"I don't see—"

"Armed!"

The single word was obstinate, a command rather than a request, but she detected concern as well.

Jacinda signed. Warmth filled her. When had he become so protective? "Very well, armed."

"I shall chose a groom and footman first thing in the morning. Each shall have a weapon with him at all times."

"As you wish."

He hesitated a moment. She thought he intended to say something more, but he merely bowed. "Good night, my dear. I shall see you in the morning."

With that he departed the room and it suddenly seemed smaller and decidedly lonely. She could still feel where his hands had gripped her. It wasn't painful, merely tingling. As she slipped from her wrapper and climbed into the large bed, she wondered what his kiss would have felt like. She blew out her candles and settled down, but her mind was unwilling to let the image of the captain go.

Back in his own chamber, Drew stood for a long time staring out the window at Chettwood's moonlit gardens. He pondered their meeting. The desire to kiss her had almost overwhelmed him but he'd feared that a kiss wouldn't have been enough. He'd wanted to run his hands over the soft flesh beneath the sheer material. But had that happened, there would have been no stopping his passion. He tamped down the image of Jacinda in his arms, knowing he would get no sleep if he allowed his imagination to have full reign. Instead, he returned to their disagreement.

The argument had been frustrating. She was, as Ben had said, the most stubborn female he'd ever encountered. A smile tipped his mouth for a moment because he realized that he rather admired her feisty nature. No doubt it had helped her to survive her ordeal of so many years away from the protection of her family. A frown creased his brow. It could get her killed if he didn't keep a close eye upon her.

This whole experience was strange. When Jacinda had first refused to marry him in London, there had been an element of relief in him. Without such a commitment, he could return to his life at sea and leave his father's estate under the new bailiff's management. He would only have to come home on occasion to see that all was as it should be. He'd always known he must wed for his family name, but after Mariah Amberly had proven herself unworthy, marriage held little appeal. He saw no need to rush into matrimony at such a young age.

It was on hearing all that had befallen Jacinda that he'd even considered honoring the betrothal his father had arranged. He certainly never wanted a bride chosen for him, but he'd accepted that he must set things right and honor that signed document. After all, what was a man if he didn't do his duty?

Yet tonight, standing in the intimacy of her bedchamber and looking at her, so sweetly innocent in garments that scarcely hid her feminine curves, it struck him that Jacinda Blanchett had become far more than his duty. He wanted to take care of her, to protect her, but most of all he wanted to possess her. But first he had to find a murderer.

Chettwood's library was a large room with floor-to-ceiling shelves filled with the finest bound books that money could buy. Few of them, however, had ever been touched except for dusting by the servants. Mr. Blanchett had been no reader, but like many men with little education and social rank, he'd seen that every great classic written had been purchased for his home. His lady wife had preferred Scott's poetic works of *Marmion* and *Lady of the Lake* and kept those volumes in her room. Cousin Millie declared she had little time for such nonsense. Mrs. Devere read only Minerva Press novels, which she kept hidden from everyone in the back of her wardrobe. Prudence and Giles had never been fond of such an idle pursuit, preferring games of all types. So the room still had the look of a lending library on its first day open to the public.

That morning, Jacinda had no time for the literary treasures that surrounded her as she sat at her father's large desk. It was the one well-used piece of furniture in the room. The fine mahogany top was covered with the estate ledgers. Her cousin and then the captain had gone over each of the books, explaining the entries. Finally, they left her to study them and become familiar with the business of such a large property. Before Drew left, he'd told her he was going to visit his father while she was occupied and urged her to stay indoors.

With a sigh, Jacinda leaned back and closed her eyes. It seemed like so much to learn. Rents and tenants, crops and drainage, livestock and fences, and, lastly, timber and orchards. It would take her another eight years to learn it all. She pushed the books away. All the figures had begun to run together. Perhaps the best way to learn was to see how everything worked firsthand, and she couldn't do that in the library. The clock on the mantelpiece read half past ten. What she needed was a tour of her holdings. She hesitated a moment, thinking of the danger the captain spoke about. Then she reminded herself that no one knew she would be out, so how could it be dangerous so soon after her arrival? She rose and went in search of Mr. Weems.

The steward had finished his rounds and was already in the estate office. As she approached, she heard the murmur of voices behind the door. She knocked and a voice bade her to enter. Inside, the man her father had trusted with his holdings stood bent over, studying something on his desk. Beside him was Libby, one of the downstairs maids, pouring a cup of coffee, gazing at him like a lovestruck child. She started when she saw Jacinda. The little maid's cheeks flushed and she backed away from the steward.

"I—I was just bringin' Mr. Weems his morning repast, ma'am." She curtsied and hurried from the room, taking one last glance at the man, who seemed

oblivious to her adoration and hadn't taken his eyes off
the paper on the desk.

Jacinda eyed the man, who straightened on realizing
who his visitor was. In her memory he had seemed quite
old, but as she looked at him now he appeared no more
than five-and-thirty. It was strange how time had played
tricks with her perspective.

"Can I help you, Mrs. Morrow?"

"Do I interrupt, Mr. Weems?"

He was handsome, if a bit weathered. Likely all the
maids were enamored of him, not just Libby. Jacinda
had few memories of him. Like most such men, he
rarely was in the manor except to discuss the estate.
What she did remembered was he'd always been kind to
her, and according to Mr. Wilkins he worked hard for
her father.

"No, madam. I was inspecting the drawing for a
cider house I've proposed we build. I spoke with Miss
Markham about it last year but she wasn't keen on the
idea due to the expense. I thought perhaps I would
show them to the captain." There was a hopeful look
on his face.

"A cider house?" She stepped forward and looked
down at the plans.

"At present we sell our apples to the local cider
houses, but we could—"

Jacinda laughed at his eager enthusiasm. It boded
well for the future of the estate management that he was
so motivated. "Such a decision cannot be made except
by Mr. Wilkins, at least until December."

A frown burrowed into brow. "December? But Miss
Markham said that once you married, the estate—"

Jacinda flushed. "She had it wrong, I fear." This pretend marriage had created problems that she'd little

taken into account. Still truly single, the estate was under the guardianship of the solicitor.

"Well, that is only five months away." The steward smiled as he rolled up the drawing. "Until then, what can I do for you, madam?"

"I was hoping that you could take me round to the tenants' cottages. I should like to meet them. To see the fields, the forest, and the livestock so that I might better understand those ledgers in the library."

His brows rose but his manner was polite. "I should be delighted. Will the captain be joining us?"

Her cheeks warmed. She was certain that Weems must think it strange that she would have need of such knowledge, but he would fully understand once everything had been revealed. "He has business to attend at his father's estate." Then Jacinda remembered her promise to the captain and the two names he'd given her at breakfast. James, the second footman, or Tobias, the under groom, were the two who would accompany her at any time. The groom would be the more fitting for this outing.

"Would you please ask Tobias to accompany us? After our inspection, I wish to go into town." She had no intention of going to town but it was easier to say she was than to explain the groom's presence.

"Tobias it shall be, ma'am." The steward put the rolled-up drawing with several other rolls in a cabinet. "I have some less expensive suggestions I should like to put forward when you are ready."

She laughed and held up her hand. "Wait until we are outdoors, then you can explain more fully. I shall go and change and meet you at the stables in fifteen minutes."

"Very good, ma'am."

As Jacinda made her way upstairs, an excitement she

had never before known coursed through her. She would be out on a horse, on her own estate, making a difference.

Returning from Rowland Park, Drew handed his hat and riding gloves to the butler. "Where is my wife, Stritch?"

"Out inspecting the estate with Weems, sir. She promised to return in time to have a light luncheon with the family at one."

The captain frowned. There could be little danger with the steward and an unplanned ride. Still, he was worried. "And the other members of the household, are they at home?"

A knowing look flashed on the butler's face. "Mr. Devere is in Wells, Mrs. Tyne and her mother are walking in the garden, and Mrs. Markham is in her room, sir."

"Thank you, Stritch." All who might wish to harm Jacinda seemed to be fully occupied, which made him feel better. "Inform me at once when my wife returns."

Drew started for the library, then stopped, "Would you have James come to me at once?"

The butler's brows rose. "Is there something I can do for you, sir?"

Afraid he might have gotten the old man's nose out of joint, Drew smiled. " 'Tis just an errand I need run and a footman is best suited to that." He would have the servant make certain Jacinda had Tobias with her.

The butler nodded, seemingly satisfied with the answer. He disappeared down the hall.

Drew made his way to the library, then smiled when he saw the stack of ledgers Jacinda had left open. Obviously she was taking her new task seriously, which was a good thing. Still, he wished she'd waited until he'd returned so that he could have ridden with her.

He settled into the chair and his thoughts turned to his visit to Rowland Park. The baron was showing progress; even the doctor was pleased. His father had actually summoned the new bailiff to his chambers to go over some of the changes Drew had given Mr. Berwick, his new steward, before they'd departed for London. Surprisingly, Lord Rowland had made few alterations to the orders. It was a good sign the old gentleman was once again taking an interest in things around him. The baron's valet had told Drew his father had requested to sit in a chair the day the bailiff visited. At this rate, Drew hoped to have his father walking by September.

A shout rang out in the hall. Its ominous timbre made a chill grip Drew. He yanked the library door open to the sight of the burly groom, Tobias, carrying Jacinda in his arms. Her face was a deathly white hue, her hat was gone and her riding habit was covered in dirt stains. Young Ben trailed behind the groom, his face so grimly set Drew almost didn't recognize him. Weems hesitated at the front door, clearly uncertain as to whether to enter or leave matters in their hands. He held Jacinda's hat in his hand.

Drew went straight to Tobias. "Give her to me, lad. Go at once for the doctor."

Jacinda slid her arms round Drew's neck , but she protested, "I don't need a doctor. 'Twas only a slight tumble from my horse. I'm only a bit shaken."

"How did this happen?" Drew looked to Weems for an explanation.

"It was an accident, Captain. We took the path along the back of the property. Someone was hunting in the next estate and a single shot flushed a covey of quail out of the bushes. The birds spooked her horse. There was nothing anyone could have done to prevent it, sir."

"He's right." Jacinda said, "If you put me down, I shall show you I can walk."

"Nonsense," Drew's grip tightened and he headed up the stairs. "Not until the doctor has seen you. Stritch," he called over his shoulder. "Send Mrs. Morrow's maid to her."

For a few minutes Drew and Jacinda were in the upper hall alone as he strode towards her room. "Are you certain it was an accident? Someone fired a gun nearby where you were riding!"

She lifted her head from his shoulder. "It was on the other side of the creek, I believe. I have heard enough gunfire to know the shot came from a good distance away. No, it was more my rusty riding skills than any bad intent. Although I must admit, I've not seen that many quail in a covey in my life. I fear I have been in the city too long."

In her apartments, Drew lay her upon the bed. She reached to rubbed at her ankle then seeing the look on his face said, "I know what you are thinking but it truly was just an accident."

Before he could comment, Martha arrived and began to fuss around her mistress. He gave the maid instructions to dress his wife for bed even while the lady protested.

Some fifteen minutes later the village physician, Dr. Fleetwood, arrived and, after a short visit with her, pronounced Mrs. Morrow to have suffered only a few minor bumps and bruises. He suggested she stay in bed for the remainder of the day.

Drew urged her to do as the doctor ordered, asked Martha to stay with her mistress all afternoon, then escorted Fleetwood to the door with profound thanks. There he found Ben waiting in the hall for him. "May I speak you with a moment, sir?

Not wanting to be overheard, they retired to the library for their conversation.

"It was no accident, Captain." Ben picked up Jacinda's black high-crown beaver hat from the desk. He put his hand inside the dome and poked his finger through a small hole that was hidden under the green ostrich feather that trimmed the stylish hat.

Someone had already made another attempt on Jacinda's life. The thought upset him so, he didn't say a thing, only walked to the window and looked out at the sunlit gardens that had seemed so welcoming. He'd thought her safe with the steward, but it seemed there would be danger everywhere until they unmasked the villain who wished to harm her.

Ben moved to stand beside the gentleman. "I shouldn't have gone down to the stables after breakfast like Jack urged me. I got distracted by the grooms who took me to the lower pasture to see the new foals and she went off with that steward. I should have been more vigilant."

Drew put a hand on the boy's shoulder. "We both got distracted with other things, but we must make certain it doesn't happen again." He sighed and crossed his arms. "What we need is a plan."

"Plan, sir? What kind of plan?"

"I don't know, but hopefully something will come to me. Until then we must make certain that one of us is with her whenever she steps outside this house."

The lad folded his arms in front of him just like Drew had. "You can count on me, Captain. I know if not for Jack, er, I mean, Jacinda, I'd be in some parish orphanage or worse, living in the rookeries of London, poor, hungry, and illiterate."

The boy barely came to Drew's shoulder, but in a fight Drew would give him good odds of winning. What he lacked in stature, he more than made up for in courage. Still he was just a lad, and Drew didn't want to put too much responsibility on him. There was also the problem of Jacinda being too cursedly independent for her own good. She'd spent too many years on her own to bend willingly to his wishes. "We must be careful that she doesn't suspect we are watching over her. I think I can be certain she would demand we not treat her like a porcelain doll."

"Bloody hell, sir, she'd wear my guts for garters if she thought I doubted she could take care of herself." He suddenly covered his mouth. "You won't tell her I said 'bloody hell,' will you? She hates when I swear."

Drew shook his head, suppressing a smile. "I won't tell her this conversation even took place." He clapped the boy on the shoulder and asked if he wanted a riding lesson since Jacinda would be in her room under the watchful gaze of her maid all afternoon.

"Would I?" Ben dashed for the door, then stopped with his hand on the knob. Guiltily he looked back at the captain. "I don't think I should be having fun what with everything that's happened."

"We must keep up normal pretenses, my boy. Jacinda is safe for now. As to the riding, you must learn now that you live in the country. She's likely to be on horseback a great deal what with estate matters and how will you keep her in sight if you cannot ride? Beside, would she not want you to enjoy yourself?"

Ben's dark eyes were troubled. "That she would, sir." But there was less eagerness as he departed.

* * *

Drew rose late the following morning. He'd found himself unable to sleep due to his worries about the wisdom of returning Jacinda to Chettwood. An attempt on her life so soon made him uncomfortable. Someone was determined. He weighed the options of taking her back to London, but in truth, she would be no safer there now that everyone knew her to be alive. Whoever wished her harm could send his henchmen there as easily as here. Near dawn he finally settled on the matter: they must make their stand here at Chettwood, where he could keep a better watch over her.

After James helped him dress, he went straight to Jacinda's room, hoping to find her taking it easy after her mishap. Unfortunately he was too late. Her maid informed him that her mistress had risen early.

"Her intention was to walk in the garden this morning, sir. 'Tis such a beautiful day." Martha gestured at the blue skies visible through the windows.

He swore under his breath. Why must she wander about in the open? A part of him didn't believe that even her enemy would be so foolish as to attack her in her own gardens, but yesterday's attempt was a sign that whoever wanted the Blanchett fortune was getting impatient.

His rapid footfalls echoed through the halls as he hurried down the stairs to the great room. She'd mentioned her mother's rose garden the first night and her desire to see how it fared, so he made his way to an alcove in the back hall that looked out over that garden. The small, sheltered area with large hew hedges surrounding three sides created an intimate atmosphere despite being outdoors. Relief filled him as he spied her with Ben, who held a basket while she cut roses. They were chatting and laughing, clearly unfazed by yesterday's events.

He savored her beauty in the fine morning mist. She looked like some delicate wood nymph come to life in a simple yellow muslin gown that ruffed in the breeze. The garment molded to a figure that had grown more alluring with the added pounds of a better diet, yet he thought his hands could still encompass her small waist. She'd cast aside her large gypsy bonnet onto a nearby stone bench and the sun glinted on her golden brown curls, creating a halo effect. His first instinct was to go to her. But he stayed the impulse. He didn't want to raise her suspicions by being overprotective. She was safe enough where she was in the little walled space.

With little to occupy him here, he settled on the bench seat at the window. He'd spent much of his free time at Chettwood searching for the will Mr. Wilkins mentioned, but had found nothing. Yet, if the solicitor's theory were true there had to be a new will. Where could it be? And who would it benefit? Giles Devere? Prudence Tyne? Mrs. Devere?

Drew had made a habit of watching the young gentleman. But Jacinda's cousin seemed more interested in meeting his friends in Wells than in what she was doing. He barely engaged her in conversation when they were together. Even Mrs. Devere and her daughter showed only polite interest in Jacinda's affairs. The answer to the mystery of Blanchett's death only seemed to slip further from his grasp with each passing day.

His reverie was interrupted by the soft murmur of voices coming from down the hall. At first he paid no heed to the conversation, continuing to watch Jacinda as she playfully gathered roses with young Ben. But as the footsteps drew nearer, the speakers' words became distinct.

"I tell you, I think she's an imposter, my dear."

Drew recognized Mrs. Devere's rather nasal voice.

"Don't be ridiculous, Mother. You have been reading too many of those silly novels. No one goes about trying to impersonate someone else." Prudence Tyne sounded impatient, as if she'd heard her mother's lament before.

"Do *you* think she looks anything like the colorless child we remember? You were scarcely more than a child yourself when she left, but I do assure you, the Jacinda Blanchett I remember was as plain as a fence post, not to mention frail and sickly. Why, this woman is . . ."

"Beautiful." The word was almost a taunt.

Mrs. Devere made a discordant sound in her throat. "If you like that sort of pushing type. Why she was positively rude to you that first day. I can tell you that her mother would turn in her grave if she thought her daughter's conduct so—"

"Perhaps I deserved it, Mama. It wasn't my place to be telling her who she can and cannot bring to her home. Honestly, Ben is a charming scamp once one gets to know him."

Drew found himself liking Mrs. Tyne, despite her tendency to flirt. He'd picked up enough from Miss Markham and the servants to know that Prudence's marriage hadn't been a happy one. Despite her mother's standoffishness, Prudence had been, if not friendly, at least polite to Jacinda.

There was a moment of silence, as if the conversation had taken a turn Mrs. Devere didn't like. She brought it back round to Jacinda. "The point is, she looks as if she's never been sick a day in her life. Although, I often thought that Millicent did the child more harm than good with her infernal cosseting."

"But, Mama, she is Jacinda, I see it in her eyes and she still has that tiny mole that Giles used to tease her about. How can you doubt her?"

The older woman harrumphed. "Well, maybe she is, but I'm not fool enough to think she and Captain Morrow are married."

"Really?" There was a hint of hope in Mrs. Tyne's voice. "Why?"

"Use your head, Prudence. He comes here looking for news of her when he first arrives in the neighborhood then returns within a week married to a woman he hardly knows. 'Tis unbelievable, betrothal papers or no. There was no need for such a rush. And Martha told my maid she was certain they don't, well . . . spend the nights together. It's a ruse, I tell you."

Drew detested the smug certainty in the woman's voice. Even more, he hated that she was right and that she'd seen through their ploy.

"You cannot know that means anything. They are strangers. Perhaps they are taking matters slowly."

"I have a woman's intuition, dear. They remain so formal and prickly. There's not the least bit of intimacy between them. They are not married, I'd wager my life on it."

"They are newlyweds still learning how to deal with one another. Besides, I well know from my own experience there are many reason for odd behaviors in wedded couples." She was quiet for a moment, then asked, "What would they gain by such a pretense?"

The strolling pair was drawing near to where Drew sat, unseen, in the alcove. He debated revealing himself to them, then thought there was no need. It was to his advantage that he could hear the unsolicited comments. He could only hope they didn't see him as they passed, for it would be difficult to explain why he hadn't shown himself.

Mrs. Devere sighed, "If you weren't forever looking at the captain like a silly green girl, it would be obvious. The marriage is for protection. As her husband, the captain would inherit if someone were to . . . well, do away with Jacinda. If everyone thinks they are married, then there is little reason to harm her."

To Drew's relief the two ladies walked past the alcove without a backward glance. They continued their leisurely pace toward the main drawing room. As they disappeared from sight, he heard Prudence say. "But that assumes money was the motive for the attack."

"'Tis my belief that Mr. Wilkins had it all wrong about her fortune being the reason. Why, Jacob Blanchett was the worst kind of profligate both before and after his marriage. More likely it was some woman he wronged who hired those men to do him in. I truly believe the old saying 'Hell hath no fury like a woman scorned' is true. I doubt Jacinda is still in danger after so many years. Still, I should not have allowed my daughter to return with the murderer still at large."

"It's rather unfortunate she has no mother or father to advise her, is it not?"

"In truth, the child is all alone if not for us." The sound of a door opening and closing told Drew that the ladies had entered the room they were bound for.

He rose and looked out at Jacinda. Softly he said, "You have it wrong, madam, Jacinda is not alone."

Drew headed straight to the rose garden where the duo greeted him. He offered to hold the basket, suggesting the lad go to the stables and have a groom saddle a horse. Drew promised he would be down for a lesson after he finished helping Jacinda with the roses.

Ben didn't need a second invitation. He thrust the basket at Drew, called a cheery good-bye to Jacinda, and disappeared down the path. Silence fell over the couple.

Uncertain where to begin, Drew at last turned to the mundane. "This is a pleasant garden." His gaze swept the area. To his surprise, he caught sight of Mrs. Devere and Prudence who had them under observation from the Gold Drawing Room. There was no better time than now to dispel any doubts about a marriage. He put the basket down on the nearby bench and stepped up to Jacinda. "How are you feeling this morning, my dear?"

"Quite well, thank you. I did assure you yesterday's incident was nothing." She smiled at him.

The watching ladies would grow bored and leave unless he took action. So without another word, he slid an arm round Jacinda's waist. The smile vanished and her eyes widened. "W-what are you doing, sir?" Her gaze remained riveted on his face but her voice was breathy, expectant.

He playfully took her chin and kissed her lightly on the mouth. She blinked up at him, uncertainty in her hazel eyes but no fear.

"Enjoying a husband's privilege."

A frown touched her brow. "Do not think you can take advantage—"

"My dear wife, do not ruin the show for your relatives. They have serious doubts as to our marriage." She attempted to turn her head and look at the manor. He tightened his hold on her chin. Then his mouth closed over hers. At first she was stiff and unyielding to his touch. He lifted his head and smiled. "My dear, I won't hurt you, I promise. Kissing can be quite pleasant if you only give it a try." There was some emotion in her eyes he couldn't define, then a glint of anger flashed. Her hand slid up behind his neck and she drew his mouth to her. This time her lips parted beneath his. The stiffness fell away from them. He pulled her yielding body to him. Unexpectedly a fire ignited deep inside Drew. The kiss deepened from show to real. He didn't care that there was someone observing them, he only cared about the woman in his arms. She was beautiful, desirable, and he wanted her.

"Captain Drew!" Ben shouted.

Drew suddenly wanted to throttle the lad behind the hedge.

"I'm saddled and ready."

Drew released Jacinda and she looked up at him. To his utter dismay, unshed tears were pooled in her eyes. "The show is over, sir." Without another word she grabbed her bonnet and the basket and hurried toward the house.

Drew stared after her. What had just happened? Ben's head appeared round the end of the hedges. "Captain, are you not ready?" The lad scanned the garden. "Is Jacinda safely inside?"

Drew looked from the manor to the lad eagerly waiting, but he couldn't leave her so upset. "I shall be with you shortly. I must have a word with Jacinda." He needed a moment to evaluate what had just happened. He'd come out to convince Mrs. Devere and Mrs. Tyne of a marriage that didn't truly exist, but somewhere during his kiss with Jacinda, he'd realized he didn't want this to be a mere play. He wanted her to be his wife. He had fallen in love with Jacinda Blanchett.

* * *

Jacinda's anger fell away as soon as she entered the cool darkness of the rear hallway. She stood a moment with her back to the door hoping to gather her wits before she faced her family. It took a moment for her to realize she was really mad at herself. Deep down inside, she'd wanted Andrew Morrow to take her in his arms and kiss her. A true, soul-baring kiss, not one for some spectacle to convince her family. Her heart ached to think the kiss had meant nothing to him but was merely a means to a goal. Worse, she'd let her anger get the better of her and kissed him like a wanton.

She put the basket on a table along with her hat, then paused to look at herself in the mirror. Her color was heightened but there was no other signs of the turmoil in her breast. What did he think of her now? She tamped down her emotions and promised herself not to wear her heart on her sleeve. When this was over she would send him on his way with her thanks. She wouldn't force him to honor their parents' wishes.

She blinked back tears and when she was more herself she retrieved the basket and set out for the kitchen to arrange the roses she'd gathered. She'd gone scarcely half the length of the long hall when Giles Devere materialized from nowhere in the rear hall as if he had been waiting for her.

"Cousin Jacinda, I have been wanting a word alone with you."

She was in no mood for whatever he had to say, still too shaken by the events in the garden. "Pray, forgive me, cousin, I am rather busy and cannot—"

A determined set transformed his round face. He reached out and grabbed her sleeve as she moved to go around. "Forgive me, cousin, but I cannot delay my request, it's most urgent. Might I trouble you for an advance on my next quarters' allowance? I've written to Mr. Wilkins but he's failed to respond so I've decided to throw myself on your mercy. Debt of honor and all."

Her gaze went to his face. In a moment of clarity, she saw the same weakness that had been said to have plagued his late father. She was well familiar with gamesters who frequented the tenements of London when a roll of the dice had left them penniless. There could be little doubt that Giles was such a one. "Cousin, you must deal with Mr. Wilkins. I fear I cannot help you for I am not yet in control of my fortune."

His mouth twisted into an ugly gash as his hand gripped at her arm. "Don't you understand. I cannot continue to game with these men if I don't pay. I know there is a strong box for estate expenses and I must—"

"Unhand my wife, sir."

Giles released her arm and stepped back as the captain came striding up the hall. "Morrow! I—I didn't hear you approach."

Jacinda was torn. A part of her was glad Drew had arrived at just that moment, yet a part of her couldn't face him after the humiliating incident in the garden.

"If your pockets are to let, Mr. Devere, you will please discuss such matters with me in the future and not harass my wife."

Giles eyed the captain warily then a cunning look came into his face. "As you wish, sir." His gaze moved back to Jacinda and, fool that he was, he did little to hide his malice. "Did I mention that I have greetings from Lady Bancroft for you? But then, you would remember her only as Miss Amberly. The earl is practically at death's door so she is most anxious to renew her acquaintance with you, her true love, I believe."

Jacinda's heart twisted. So the squire's daughter wanted to renew old ties. She glanced at the captain's face but it was an unreadable mask. Did he still harbor feelings for his first love? A throbbing started at the back of Jacinda's eyes and she suddenly realized she needed to go to her room. "Forgive me, but I have had too much sun and fear my head aches."

The captain took the basket of roses and shoved them at Giles. "Deliver these to the housekeeper then await me in the library. Jacinda, allow me to escort you to your room."

Giles seemed to fade away and the captain took her arm and escorted her up the stairs. At her door, he softly said, "I would speak with you when you are feeling better, my dear."

She turned to face him. "You need not worry that I shall hold you to the terms of those old betrothal documents, sir. I know that I have the right of refusal on my twenty-first birthday and I shall exercise that right."

His green eyes scanned her face for a moment as if trying to read the meaning of her words. "We needn't discuss that at this time. But what I must tell you—" he reached out for her, but she opened the door and stepped inside.

"I would only ask that you be discreet while everyone thinks we are married." She went to close the door, but Captain Morrow hand stopped her. He angrily stepped inside.

"Have I given you reason to think that I am such a cad, Jacinda?" His wounded pride was written on his face.

She shook her head ever so slightly, for it was beginning to hurt in earnest. "But you have also not seen the woman you loved for eight years. You might think differently once you meet. I don't want to keep—"

"The woman I love? Do you mean Mariah? You have it—"

But before the captain could finish Millicent Markham appeared at the doorway. "Oh, Captain, young Ben is below asking for you." Her cousin's gaze lit on Jacinda and she hurried forward. "Why, child, you are looking burnt to the socket. Have you the headache?" When Jacinda nodded, the older woman bustled about, shooing the captain from the room. "I shall take good care of her, sir. She'll be her old self by supper."

Before the captain knew what had happened he'd been ushered from the room, the door closed in his face. He'd come to tell Jacinda he loved her but he'd been unable to utter a word before he'd found his honor under attack. As if Mariah Amberly had meant a thing to him in a long time. He wanted to clear up the misunderstanding but he could see she was unwell. Jacinda was under a great deal of pressure from all sides. Perhaps it wasn't the best time to reveal his feeling for her. He would be better served finding who wished to harm her.

An angry glint rose in his eyes. The first person he would handle was Giles Devere. Drew strode off to the library.

CHAPTER SEVEN

After a rocky start, their first week at Chettwood Manor passed quietly. Jacinda and the captain settled into a formal but friendly accord after she apologized for her comment. She blamed it on her headache and he politely accepted her excuse, not pressing her for further explanation. Still, she'd come to realize her insinuations had stemmed from jealousy. Yet she was afraid to search her soul too much for the answer to why Mariah Amberly, who'd enchanted Andrew so long ago, could engender such an ignoble emotion in Jacinda. She tried instead to focus on the reason she'd come home: to find her father's killer.

But nothing of note happened. Many of their nearest neighbors came to call, but Jacinda remembered few of them, not having been out of the nursery when they used to visit. It was clear they were more interested in where she had been for eight years than in speaking about what they knew of her father. In truth, they appeared as puzzled as she as to what had happened; although several discreetly warned her that where money was involved, it was always best to be wary of one's relations.

As the days passed without progress in ferreting out any information or anything of note happening, Jacinda grew impatient. Her life and her feelings for the captain were on hold until this mystery was solved. She was forced into close contact with the gentleman and that only made her attraction for him grow. It certainly would make it more difficult in the end, when he walked away to resume his own life.

Something had to be done. Something that would draw out the guilty party. She put her mind to the problem and finally one afternoon a plan came to her. A very dangerous plan. But the most difficult part would be convincing Captain Morrow and Ben to go along with her suggestion.

It took her a day to gather the courage to confront the gentleman. She had little doubt that he wasn't going to like what she proposed. There was also the strange feeling she got in her stomach each time he was around. She found herself wanting more and more to be with him, to have him smile at her and to have him look at her with those green eyes that seemed to smolder at times with an intensity that ignited something deep inside her. She was rapidly losing the battle with her heart despite knowing his feelings for Mariah.

Finally, late that afternoon nearly ten days after their arrival, she went down to the stables and found Ben and the captain just finishing a riding lesson in the paddock.

"I must speak with you both, alone."

There was no quibbling. Ben pointed to the gazebo on the lake, then raced ahead with a handful of grain to toss at the ducks. Jacinda and Drew strolled after him in silence. Ben and the captain settled on the gazebo stairs, the golden glow of the fading sun bathing them in an orange sheen.

Jacinda paced in front of them until she gathered her nerve and began. "After a week and a half of subtle questioning, it's obvious that none of the servants knows anything about the events of the night my father and I were attacked. As for the family, if they know something, they aren't talking. So I think we should take a more aggressive tack."

The captain frowned. "Aggressive? What do you mean?"

"I think I should . . .well, I should begin riding out alone to lure the killer to action."

"Absolutely not!" The captain came off the stairs to stand face-to-face with her. "You may as well hang a target on your back."

"Not if you and Ben are out there protecting me." Seeing the denial in his face, she hurriedly said, "Pray listen before you refuse, I know it will be dangerous but it's the only way I can think to lure this person out into the open.

The gentleman paced to the shore and back, his angry tones carrying over the water. Even the ducks were frightened by the loud disturbance and swam to the far side of the lake. "Do you have any idea how many things could go wrong? How many trees there are to hide behind? You would be like . . . like one of those ducks—completely vulnerable." He gestured at the mallards who had no protection on the open water.

"I'm not afraid and I won't take any unnecessary chances. Besides, I'm tired of doing nothing. We could be here another eight years waiting for whoever it is to make another attempt. This isn't just about me. I want my father's killer brought to justice." She glared at him, determined to make him accept the plan. They argued for another ten minutes, each unwilling to give in to the other.

In frustration, at last she shouted, "If you don't agree,

I see no reason to go on with this ruse of a pretend marriage. I shall handle things my own way and you can return to your father's estate for good."

Captain Morrow froze at her words. He turned to look at Ben, who'd been quite willing to allow the gentleman to handle the argument.

The lad's mouth puckered a moment, then he said, "We must tell her, sir, before she does something completely foolish."

Jacinda's cheeks flushed warmly. She'd lost her temper and behaved badly. "Tell me what?"

The captain straightened. "We didn't want to alarm you, but the accident on your first day back at Chettwood was no accident."

She shook her head. "But I told you—"

"I know what you told us. But have you taken a look at the hat you wore that day?"

Jacinda looked from the captain to Ben and back as cold icy fingers played along her spine. "What about my hat?"

Ben rose and came to her. "There's a bullet hole underneath the feathers. We found it that night. The only reason it wasn't knocked from your head was because of that sheer netting that you tie around your neck when you wear it. That shot was aimed at you, not the birds."

Jacinda's knees grew weak. Somehow in the back of her mind, she'd almost convinced herself it wasn't true that someone wanted her dead. But now it seemed there was indisputable proof.

The captain came to her, taking her shoulders in his hands. "Jacinda, promise me you won't take any unnecessary risks. Especially not this foolish plan you have just proposed."

She looked up into worried eyes and knew he only

wanted what was best for her. She nodded her head, but she was suddenly feeling extremely vulnerable. He pulled her into his arms and laid his head atop hers. In a hushed voice he said, "We won't let anything happen to you, my dear."

Jacinda felt safe and protected in his embrace. She wished she didn't ever have to move from that spot beside the lake. After a moment the gentleman released her and a chill seemed to settle permanently inside her.

Drew gave her a reassuring smile. "I think we must return to the manor or we shall be late for supper. I wouldn't want to incur your Cousin Millie's wrath."

Jacinda forced herself to return his smile but she was unable to sustain the gesture and it slipped from her face. She couldn't get past the news they'd just given her. She'd been shot at. Somehow that night long ago seemed like a child's nightmare, but this had just confirmed the truth: that someone still very much wanted her dead.

Ben slipped up beside her and slid his hand into hers. "If you want to leave here, I'll go with you, Jack. We could go back to London or someplace far away. I'm old enough to work and take care of us."

She looked back at the manor. It had been her home for the first twelve years of her life. It was her father's legacy to her and that was worth fighting for. Her father's death must not have been in vain. "Chettwood will be mine and I intend to stay and find out the truth." She looked at the captain and felt the fool for her conduct. "Will you forgive my childish threat and stay as well?"

He smiled and drew her arm through his. "I am here until the very end, my dear."

Her fingers tightened on his arm and a feeling of

strength seemed to flow from him to her. A quiet calm came over her. She wouldn't think about the day that would come all too soon when he would leave to return to his life at sea. She would only savor their time together. "Shall we go? We don't want to keep the others waiting."

At luncheon the following day, Stritch had begun to serve when a commotion sounded at the front door announcing visitors at Chettwood. Within minutes a footman ushered Mr. Wilkins and Mr. Matthew Blanchett into the dining room, where everyone but Ben was gathered. One of the grooms had taken him fishing, with the captain's approval, and Cook had packed the lads a picnic. Ben had never been on a picnic before and Jacinda hoped it would be only one of many he'd enjoy here at Chettwood.

She rose to greet the gentlemen. A twinge of sadness stirred within her, for her uncle looked a great deal like her father. "Uncle Matthew, how good to see you."

Matthew Blanchett, sixty, with thinning auburn hair and a long glum face, looked flustered as he took his niece in his arms. "I'm hoping you will say the same after I impart the bad news I bring."

She drew back, and searched his face. "What has happened? Is it Jane? Claude?" She hadn't seen her Blanchett cousins in years but they were family.

A look passed between the newly arrived gentlemen, but Uncle Matthew could only shake his head. Jacinda was suddenly afraid that the news was going to be very bad.

Millicent Markham stepped up. "Mr. Blanchett, Jacinda seems to have forgotten her manners. May we present her husband, Captain Morrow." The gentlemen exchanged bows and Millie said, "Won't you join us?"

The solicitor and Mr. Blanchett gladly accepted and Stritch sent for two more place settings. But it was clear something was weighing on Matthew Blanchett, for he'd scarcely settled at the edge of a chair when he began. "There is no easy way to tell you this, my dear. I fear the business is finished."

"The business?" Jacinda blinked, startled that his uneasiness was about business and not some life-or-death matter.

Mr. Wilkins pushed his spectacles up on the bridge of his nose even as he eyed the loaded tray of cucumber sandwiches a footman brought round. "That is perhaps a bit melodramatic, but I think what your uncle is trying to tell you is that it will be years, if ever, before there will be any profits from the foundry."

A gasp went up in the room. Giles, who'd been toying with a piece of fruit with a bored expression on his face, sat up. "What the devil have you done, sir?"

Matthew Blanchett stiffened and his eyes narrowed as they took in Giles's pale green jacket with large gold buttons and waistcost with delicate green leaves. "I don't believe this is any of your affair, young man." He turned back his niece. "Jacinda, perhaps we should retire to the library to finish this discussion after we have dined."

To everyone's surprise, Captain Morrow spoke from his position at the head of the table. "I think the entire family should hear this, sir. After all, if I take your meaning, my wife will no longer be able to provide the level of income to her family that her father once did."

Mr. Wilkins nodded, even while he selected a second sandwich from the tray which sat on the table in front of him. "That is exactly what your uncle is saying. Mrs. Morrow, as your father's executor, I shall be forced to make some difficult choices due to the unfortunate circumstance that Blanchett Foundry burned to the ground two days ago."

Jacinda sat stunned. Every fiber of her being wanted to throw herself into the captain's arms for reassurance and comfort. But she wouldn't be so weak. She gathered her wits and asked, "Tell me, sir, that no one was hurt."

Uncle Matthew nodded. "Thankfully not, my dear. I cannot tell you—"

Mrs. Devere shoved her plate away from her. "What kind of adjustments to our income are you speaking of, sir?" Her dark gaze locked on the solicitor, who seemed more interested in eating than in informing them of the crisis.

After swallowing, he smiled sheepishly. "Forgive me, but we were in such haste we have not eaten since dawn." He brushed the crumbs from his waistcoat then said, "I've looked over your affairs, Mrs. Morrow. Much of your father's income was used up when Mr. Blanchett and your father decided to refit the foundry some nine years ago. There were mortgages taken out and debts incurred. Since that time, the profits have been, shall we say, spotty due to the fact that your father allowed his brother to make certain investments with the income before profits were dispersed." The solicitor cast Mr. Blanchett an accusatory look before he continued. "Along with that, I've expended a great deal of money at Bow Street hiring runners to help in the search for your father's killer with few results." The gentleman looked at the captain. "And of course, I have paid out the remainder of the settlement to Lord Rowland that was agreed upon by Jacinda's father."

A frown appeared on the captain's face. "You did?"

The solicitor nodded. "Sent the check express on Monday."

The captain fell silent again.

"Mr. Wilkins," Jacinda said, "are you telling me that I am without funds?" For herself, she wasn't frightened since she'd been without funds since before Trudy died. But Jacinda had an entire estate full of people depending on her, tenants and family alike.

"Not nearly as bad as that, my dear." His kind gaze settled on her. "The estate is yours and while the income is modest, it will see you through. As to your dependents," the old gentleman looked to the Deveres. "I shall be forced to reduce their income to fifty pounds per annum, each."

"Fifty pounds!" Mrs. Devere shrieked. "Why that is no better than what a governess might expect. We shan't be able to get by on that amount! Why, we've scarcely gotten by on what little we did receive. Jacinda, you cannot allow him to do that! Giles must live like his friends, like a gentleman. How can he do that on a paltry fifty pounds a year!" The lady fell to hysterically weeping.

Prudence hurried round the table to her mother's side, her face pink from embarrassment at the lady's outburst. "Mama, I do assure you that we can make do. We have little expense here. It's not Jacinda's fault." Mrs. Tyne gripped her mother's hand, but the lady was too distraught to control her emotions and soon Prudence was forced to ask that they be excused. She led her sniffling mother away.

Jacinda put her cup down, for she had no taste for food or drink at the moment. "Mr. Wilkins, surely there is some way I can better provide for my aunt and cousins?"

"I fear you cannot, my dear. However, I made several inquiries on Devere's behalf about positions in London and I am certain I could find him a post with one of the lords who are active in Parliament." The solicitor nodded at Giles.

"Live in London!" The young man's eyes brightened on that final word. Then he slumped back. "Mama would never allow me to take such a post. She will think it beneath me. She is always reminding me that were if not for my three Devere cousins in Kent, I should be a viscount."

Mr. Wilkins's brows rose at that odd bit of nonsense but he merely said, "I shall speak to her at supper this evening when she is calmer. I am certain that Jacinda will be perfectly happy to continue to house your mother and sister here."

Jacinda agreed she would and surprisingly, Giles seemed quite content. He began to make inroads in the food on his plate. Jacinda, with little hunger, pushed her plate aside and excused herself. Cousin Millie offered to see her to her room, but Jacinda insisted that she remain and finish her lunch. The captain rose to escort her to the door. There he kissed her hand. For Jacinda it seemed a strangely intimate moment even in a room full of people.

"I will stay and play host to our guests, my dear. And don't worry, this estate is sound. It will provide all that you need."

Jacinda stared into his green eyes. She couldn't quite explain, but she took comfort from his confidence. She was too overwhelmed at the moment to think clearly. She bid him good afternoon and departed to her room to gather her wits and to rest.

* * *

The gold drawing room stood empty that evening when Jacinda arrived to await the others and the summons for supper. Being early, she strolled to the set of double doors that opened onto the terrace. It was a lovely evening that had cooled from the day's warmth. A soft breeze from the west ruffled her curls but she didn't care, for the scent of gardenia it carried was so pleasant. The colorful array of roses, peonies, and larkspur beckoned her, so she strolled out into the gardens to enjoy the peaceful evening.

She wondered if her Aunt Devere would be joining them for supper. Surely by now the lady's shattered nerves had been calmed and she'd accept the changes in her circumstances. With Giles working, they would be far better off than before. Such a post would certainly make Jacinda feel less guilty about the reduction in funds the solicitor would soon be making.

She came to the gate at the end of the garden. Looking back, she could see that the drawing room remained empty so she moved through the gate and crossed the path into the rear garden. But she discovered that garden was occupied. Her Aunt Devere and Prudence were having a heated discussion while they sat on a bench. Jacinda hesitated a moment and watched the ladies. Prudence seemed to grow frustrated and threw up her hands. Without a backward glance, she hurried back to the manor, leaving her mother alone. Not wanting to intrude on her clearly agitated aunt, Jacinda veered up the path towards the stables instead.

As she moved along the gravel path, she determined that she would push all her worries about the Deveres from her mind for the night. Her gaze was drawn to the pasture, where the shorthorn cattle, newly delivered from Yorkshire, were grazing. They had been a suggestion of Weems during her first days at Chettwood, and, with her cousin's council, they decided to purchase the stock with the funds from the strongbox. It occurred to her that Millicent had maintained the estate quite well, but there had been few improvements or innovations. Her father had never really worked to make the estate profitable due to his income from the foundry, and her cousin had very much followed his pattern. But that didn't mean she couldn't make Chettwood provide a good income once she gained control. The captain had assured her it was possible.

A certainty that she would manage settled over her. There had been a part of her that had dreaded coming back home. It had been the thought of being useless and sheltered once again after so many years of taking care of herself. The loss of the foundry made her realize that there would be a great deal to do. The estate could be brought up to its full potential.

A loud shout echoed in the growing darkness. She turned in the direction of the stable, aware that was where it had come from. She hurried to see what had happened. She'd only gone some ten yards when Tobias came running up the path towards her.

"Mrs. Morrow! Mrs. Morrow!" The name always triggered feelings of guilt that she was being untruthful with her relatives. "Mrs. Morrow, there's been an accident. It's Ben. He's taken a bad fall. I told them lads not to go up in that loft but they snuck up the ladder after the other grooms went home for the night. I was out back unloadin' bales of straw from the wagon what were just delivered."

Jacinda couldn't breathe for a moment. Ben couldn't

be seriously hurt. One important reason for coming home was to bring him to a place that was safe. She lifted her skirts and hurried after the groom.

Two lanterns illuminated the main aisle of the stable. In the soft glow of light Ben lay still in the fresh straw at the foot of the loft ladder. Cal, one of the stable lads who'd taken him fishing, knelt beside him. Above the boys she could see a ladder rung hanging loose, as if it had given way beneath Ben's weight. She arrived at his side and could see he was in pain. A large lump had begun to swell at the side of his head.

"How badly are you hurt?"

His attempt to grin twisted into a grimace, and a deep groove etched his brow. "Cal and I just wanted to see the kittens. Owww—" he groaned and grabbed at his head.

"Never mind about that. We must take you to the house." Jacinda ran her hands along both arms and legs to search for broken bones. He winched when she got to his right ankle.

"My leg and head hurt the most." Jacinda saw a hole torn in his breeches. Blood stained the edges of the tattered material. He would survive but needed a doctor.

She brushed the hair from his forehead and kissed him beside the swelling. "Never fear, we shall have you feeling better before you sleep."

The lad nodded his head and tested the growing lump. "Just my luck to fall in the summer. If only there was some icicles about to keep the swelling down, like when I tumbled down the Wapping stairs last December, I'd be right as rain in the morning."

Jacinda remembered the incident well. She'd been furious with him for being out after dark. But that had been quickly forgotten when a kind Russian sailor had brought the injured lad home. In his broken English, he had suggested they pull icicles from the eaves above their window to use to reduce the swelling and pain. It had worked.

That memory triggered an idea. "We have an ice-house here, but I cannot be certain there is still ice this late in the season." She rose and looked at the man and boy who awaited her orders. "Cal, run ahead and have Stritch send to Westbury for the doctor. Tobias, carry Ben to his room. I'll go to the icehouse and see what I can find." She moved aside as the large groom stepped in and scooped up Ben.

"Jack, don't go there alone, it's not safe." The lad looked over the groom's shoulder as they started up the aisle.

"Don't worry. The icehouse is only twenty yards or so into the woods at the back of the west pasture. It will only take a moment and I shall be there and back before the doctor can come from the village."

Before Ben could say more, Tobias carried the lad out the stable doors.

Alone, Jacinda helped herself to one of the lanterns and an empty water bucket. She hurried from the stables, making her way to the icehouse.

Heading out the rear door, she passed the partially un-loaded straw wagon, crossed the meadow in the fading light, and entered the woods. The lantern's light held back the night as she stepped under the canopy of trees. Even in the lonely woods, her thoughts were on Ben. Hopefully all his injuries were superficial and he would be back on his feet in no time.

The lantern's light soon caught the gray stone walls of the icehouse, built sometime in the previous century by a former owner of the estate. It was a rather large building but she knew that its interior was much smaller, the walls being some three feet thick. The icehouse looked much like the tenant cottages except for a few differences, most notably that the roof came to within two feet of the ground. This was due to the fact that much of the interior was underground; a man-made cave, as it were. Secondly, there wasn't a single window. And lastly, a set of narrow steps went up the wall and along the sloping roof to the peak, where a heavy trapdoor had been fashioned into the slate tiles so that it was barely visible.

The trapdoor was only used during the winter, when ice was cut from the lake and brought to be stored. She opened the lower door, which would give her access to the main storage area. She held the lantern up and illuminated a set of stone steps leading downward to a second door at the bottom. Much like in a mine shaft, wooden beams arched about the passageway to hold the stones in place. Jacinda stepped into the stairwell, taking the time to close the outside door behind her. That done, she descended. The air around her became notably cooler and there was a damp smell of wet stone. Hopefully this meant there was ice left from last March's harvest. She opened the second door and stepped onto a wooden platform some ten feet above the floor in a small room. The sound of dripping water echoed in the open space. She could see a set of wooden stairs on the far wall that went to the ceiling, where the underside of the trapdoor could be seen.

In one corner, the bright glint of ice reflected the lantern light. Ice picks hung on the wall at the bottom of the stairs. She made her way down, noting water on the floor from the constant melting. She grabbed a pick from the peg where it hung and made her way over slippery stones to what ice remained.

She set her lantern on the floor and the pail she'd brought beside one of the remaining chunks, and began to pick at the ice. It broke quite easily due to the long time in storage. Hopefully, Stritch could find some oil cloth to keep the water from saturating Ben's bed, or perhaps a bowl would do.

She'd just put the last large piece of ice in the full pail when a thump and shattering glass sounded on the door at the top of the platform. Someone or something was behind that door. All her fears about returning to Chettwood rushed back. She'd been a fool to come out here alone. Someone must have been watching her every move to know she was here. Her grip tightened on the ice pick.

Jacinda grabbed her lantern and climbed up the stairs, then hung the lantern beside the door. Taking a deep breath and positioning the ice pick to repel an attack, she wrenched opened the door.

Flames leapt out at her. An inferno consumed the entire stairway. Someone had stuffed a bale of straw in the passageway, then tossed a lit lantern on top of it. The narrow stairway was completely impassable and worse, the old wooden beams were on fire. Someone was trying to burn the place down with her inside.

Just then movement caught her eye. Jacinda realized the upper door was wide open. A white face stared down at her with satisfaction. How could it be? Jacinda shouted over the crackling flames. "Aunt Devere, why?"

A strange, demented look settled in the lady's eyes. "It should have all belonged to my Prudence." With no explanation, the lady disappeared into the darkness.

Jacinda backed into the main ice room, horrified at

what was happening. Seeing no hope for escaping up the stairwell, she turned and spied the wooden stairs across the room. Hope filled her as she raced for them. She no longer needed her lantern since the flaming doorway lit the room.

In the ceiling above her the heat and smoke pooled, but she held her breath and climbed upward. She reached the trap door, but the smoke was so thick she could barely see. She ran her hand over the wood, but found no latch. Her eyes watered and she coughed, but she pulled her skirt up to cover her face, then pushed with all her might against the wooden portal. To her horror it refused to open. There must have been a latch on the outside.

The smoke grew so thick that she edged back down the stairs and watched the rapidly spreading fire below her. The wooden steps at the inner door were being slowly eaten by flames, while others were inching up the beams toward the ceiling.

Fear gave her strength to rush the trapdoor once again, but to no avail. It remained shut tight. Within seconds the smoke was unbearable, forcing Jacinda to move back to the bottom of the stairs. Out of ideas, she stood with her back to the cool stone wall and watched the fire spreading. Certainty that she would die filled her. Tears rolled down her cheeks as she wondered what would happen to Ben. Instinctively she knew that Captain Morrow would make certain he was cared for even if her family would not.

As the captain's face came to her mind, a pain pierced her heart. She loved him. She didn't know for certain when the respect had turned to love but as she faced certain death, she knew that she loved him with all her being. She could only pray that he wouldn't blame himself that they'd failed to unmask Aunt Devere as the killer. She loved him and would never be able to tell him, never!

A loud crack sounded and the burning door frame shifted and fell onto the platform that groaned under the heavy weight. Jacinda slid down the wall to the wet floor and covered her face. She didn't want to watch the fire's steady progress up the beams.

CHAPTER EIGHT

Drew tugged at his cravat as he hurried down the stairs. He'd spent the afternoon handling correspondence from his ship about his return. He'd also written the head of Bow Street regarding a request for information about the Blanchett investigation. Last, he'd jotted notes to send to Berwick, his father's new steward. When he'd finally gotten to his room, James was nowhere to be found, so he'd had to manage on his own. Now he was late and hoped he hadn't kept the others waiting long.

He'd just reached the front hall when the front door opened and Tobias stepped inside with an injured Ben in his arms. The groom was clearly looking for someone to tell him what to do, for he stopped and looked in search of a household servant to take over the boy's care.

Drew went straight to the boy and lifted his hair to inspect the swelling above his eye. "What happened?"

Ben reached out and grabbed the gentleman's lapel. "I took a tumble, Captain, but that ain't important. Jack's gone on an errand to the icehouse." He tugged at the coat the better to make his point. "It ain't safe, and I told her so, sir."

Drew quickly inspected the lad's limbs and, finding

no broken bones, ordered Tobias to take Ben to his room. "I'll go find her, lad. Where is this icehouse?"

Tobias gestured with a nod of his head. "Go to the stables, sir. Out beyond the carriage house in the west meadow ye'll find a path through the trees. Ye need a lantern to show ye the way in the dark. Take one from the stables."

Anger stirred in Drew as he made his way to the stables. What had she been thinking to go off alone? Short of locking her in her room, he was his wit's end as to what to do. Hopefully no one would expect her to be out after dark. He wouldn't be comfortable until she was at his side. There was no moonlight due to an approaching storm. By the time he reached the stables, a strange disquiet overtook him. The double doors to the building opened to a black void. He could hear the horses nickering and moving about in their stalls. Both lanterns that usually lit the main aisle were gone. A sense of foreboding took hold of him.

He moved toward the meadow, picking up his pace. Coming round the end of the large building, light flickered in the woods. At first, he thought it was Jacinda's lantern, but as he drew near the trees, he saw flames licking the side of a building. He cried, "FIRE! FIRE IN THE WOODS!" He could only hope someone would heard him. If the woods caught fire, it might get out of control and burn the carriage house, stables, and even the manor.

He raced through the woods to the burning building. The only door was engulfed in flames. "JACINDA!" he shouted.

For a moment he thought he heard laughter in the woods, but decided it was only the wind. He moved closer to the fiery doorway. "JACINDA!"

Through the crackling flames he heard a muffled cry.

He moved so close to the flames he was forced to lift his arm for protection from the searing heat. "JACINDA, WHERE ARE YOU?"

The faint echoed up the passageway, "I'm down here, Captain! Help!"

His first instinct was to hurl himself down the flaming stairway to reach her. But foolish bravery would do neither of them any good. Logic told him there had to be another way inside. Drew ran to the back of the building where he found a stairway to the roof. He climbed the stairs two at a time until he reached the top. He slid back the bolt, nearly ripping the heavy trapdoor from it hinge when he threw it open. Smoke and heat boiled out, forcing him back. He couldn't see anything. "JACINDA, UP HERE."

Fearful that she had fallen unconscious in the thick smoke, Drew tied his handkerchief over his nose and mouth, then hoisted himself onto the trapdoor ledge. He dropped his legs over the edge, preparing to jump into the dense smoke. But before he could enter, Jacinda's head appeared out of the billowing cloud. Despite having her face covered with layers of her silk skirt, she was coughing and struggling to breathe.

He lifted her out and joined her on the stairs, pulling her up into his arms. Tugging the kerchief from his face he asked, "Are you unharmed?"

She nodded, unable to say a word due to her coughing. He swept up into his arms and carried her down the narrow stairs to the ground. Behind him there was a sudden shift as the lower door frame collapsed and a shower of sparks swirled into the sky. Worried that the entire building would soon fall, he moved to the edge of the trees but stayed within the clearing. At a safe distance, he put her on her feet, but kept her in his arm as he used the kerchief to wipe the tears and soot from her face. After a moment, he kissed her forehead. "My dear Jacinda, I thought I had lost you before I got the chance to tell you that I love you."

Jacinda's eyes widened despite tears that streamed down her cheeks. She was still too choked up from the smoke to speak, but her face softened. She took his hands in hers and laid her cheek upon them to convey the message she was unable to speak at the moment. His grip tightened and he turned her hands over to kiss them. She winced and he saw the blistered skin on the back of one.

"You're hurt."

She managed to choke out in a raspy voice, "Only . . . only a little. 'Tis nothing when I think what might have happened if not for you." She reached up and touched his cheek. He smiled and kissed her lightly on the lips. As much as he wanted to kiss her breathless, now wasn't the time. The roof of the icehouse burst into flames. "How did this happen?"

Before she could say a word, the sound of running footsteps echoed in the woods. Weems, along with several footmen, grooms, and gardeners appeared on the path carrying water buckets and shovels. The steward shouted orders and the men fanned out and began to fight the fire. Seeing the pair in the firelight, Weems came to where the captain and Jacinda stood.

"We heard your cries, sir, are you both unharmed?"

The captain nodded, unable to draw his gaze from the all-consuming fire. "You cannot save the place, just keep the fire from spreading into the woods." He looked at Jacinda, who appeared pale in the flickering firelight.

"I'm taking my wife to the manor. I'm certain you can handle this without us, Weems."

"Very good, sir." Weems hurried back to lend a hand.

Drew led Jacinda back through the woods. The brightly lit manor seemed to beckon them from the darkness. Occasionally he dropped a kiss atop her hair to reassure himself that she was truly safe in his arms. At the garden gate, they could see members of the household standing on the terrace dressed for supper, staring at the glow from the woods.

Cousin Millie hurried down the steps to meet them. When she saw Jacinda, the lady cried, "What happened, child?"

Drew didn't release his hold on his love. He kept moving in the direction of the drawing room door, for he sensed her strength was almost spent. "Jacinda was trapped in the icehouse after someone set it afire."

There was a collective gasp from those on the terrace. Drew scanned the waiting group. Thomas Wilkins stood with a glass of sherry beside a frowning Matthew Blanchett. Prudence and Giles lingered at the edge of the light that spilled from the drawing room, their moods somber. Everyone moved aside as Drew led Jacinda into the room. He insisted she sit down upon a chaise until they heard her story. He'd barely gotten her settled when Prudence handed him a glass of claret for Jacinda.

"We must get the child to her room," Millie declared, horrified at the soot-blackened gown and traces of grime on Jacinda's face.

Drew gave Jacinda a searching look. The color seemed to be returning to her cheeks as she sipped at the drink. They needed to know what had happened.

"Can you stay a few minutes, my dear? Long enough to tell us how the fire started?"

Jacinda nodded. She finished the claret before she told her story. "I went to the icehouse to get ice chips for Ben's ankle. Oh, dear, how is he?"

Cousin Millie shook her head. "He has a few scrapes and bruises. He'll have a limp for a few days and will have the headache but it's nothing to worry about, child."

Uncle Matthew sat down in the chair opposite, never taking his gaze from his niece's face. "You went to the icehouse, and then?"

Jacinda's cheeks flamed pink and she developed a sudden interest in the burned spot on her hand. "I was getting ice when I heard a crash and discovered that . . . that Aunt Devere had thrown a bale of straw into the stairway then tossed a lantern atop it." She looked up at Drew and seemed to gain strength. At last she said the difficult words. "She tried to kill me."

Giles stepped forward. "That a bloody lie! My mother would never do such a thing!"

"Stubble it, boy." Matthew put out a hand to hold the young man back, frowning at him. "We must hear everything."

Giles pressed his lips closed but continued to glower at Jacinda. Prudence put a calming hand on her brother's arm . . . or perhaps it was to show a united front to those in the room. Her motivation was unclear to Drew.

The solicitor removed his spectacles and began to clean them with his kerchief. "Are you sure it was your aunt?"

Jacinda nodded. "She spoke to me. She said, 'It all should have belonged to Prudence'."

"Oh, dear God." Horror etched Matthew Blanchett's face. His gaze moved to lock on Prudence Tyne.

The young widow's face flushed red. "I—I don't understand. Why would my mother think that Uncle Jacob's fortune should be mine?"

Mr. Blanchett slumped back in his chair. It was as if he were seeing her for the first time. He shook his head as if disappointed that his worst fears had been realized. "I always suspected, but never asked him or your mother."

Prudence's face grew pale and her hand trembled as she clutched at her brother. "Suspected what, sir?"

"That you were my brother's natural daughter."

She shook her head and began to back away from them. "It cannot be true. Mama would never have betrayed Papa in such a way. Never!"

Matthew rubbed a hand over his tired eyes, then stared at her with pity etched on his face. "When my brother was in negotiations with the viscount to wed Jacinda's mother, he met Iris Devere. She was young and beautiful, with a husband more interested in gaming than in his young wife and child. You cannot deny that your father rarely spent time at home. No doubt Iris was flattered by my brother's attentions. I warned him he was playing with fire, but when it came to women my brother had a weakness, like some men have for spirits or gaming. He just couldn't resist a beautiful woman and your mother was quite a beauty in her day."

Silence filled the room for a moment. For Jacinda it was a startling revelation. She loved her father, but she'd scarcely known his true self. Seeing the look on Prudence's face, Jacinda rose and went to take her newly discovered half-sister in her arms. But the widow stepped back, fending her off. "No, I—I must find my mother. I must ask her." She dashed from the room, then her slippered footsteps could be heard tapping on the stairs. Giles glared angrily around the room, then went after her . . . or, more likely, to his room to sulk.

Jacinda returned to Drew, who slid his arm round her shoulders. He whispered into her ear. "Don't be hurt, she is a bit shattered by the news. I'm certain she will come around."

Jacinda questioned Millie whether she'd ever had any inkling of Prudence's paternity.

The older woman flushed. "Well, I did notice that Mrs. Devere acted very ungrateful to your father for the home he provided her and the children. But I suppose by the time they came to Chettwood she was well over her infatuation. They say that love and hate are opposite sides of the same coin, not that I know—"

Running footsteps echoed in the great hall. Within a minute, a breathless Giles appeared in the doorway. "Mama is not in her room."

The image of her aunt's angry countenance flashed in Jacinda's mind. "I could scarcely see Aunt Devere through the flames but it appeared as if she ran deeper into the forest and not toward the manor. She must still be out there."

Mr. Wilkins, who'd moved to stand by the drinks table, gazed out into the darkness. "We must find her, for it is likely to storm before dawn. I, for one, would like to hear what she has to say about her actions tonight and about your father's death." He turned to Jacinda, a rueful expression on his face. "My dear, I must ask your forgiveness."

"Why, sir?"

"I've had it wrong all these years. It wasn't about the inheritance. She killed him out of revenge and hate."

Jacinda's face reflected her shock. "My aunt hired those men who accosted us."

The solicitor's look challenged Giles to deny the charge he was about to make. "Can there be any doubt she hired those men to kill Mr. Blanchett? I'm hoping if we handle her properly, she'll confess it all."

Matthew Blanchett rose and moved to the terrace doorway. "We must organize a search party for your mother, Mr. Devere. Summon any servants not fighting the fire."

With one last angry glance at the others, Giles departed for the kitchens. Mr. Blanchett arched a questioning brow at the solicitor, who reluctantly put down his glass and joined the gentleman at the door. "Captain, if you would put my niece in the hands of her maid, we could use your help." The gentlemen disappeared out the door, pulling up their collars as the misting rain began.

Reluctant to leave, Drew pulled Jacinda into his arms. "It's over, my love. You're safe at last. You can finally get on with your life." Mutual adoration reflected in their eyes.

She blushed and stammered, "I-I cannot thank you enough for all your help."

His grin widened as he kissed her lips. "I can think of a way."

Wonder and hope filled her face. "Whatever can I do?"

"You can marry me, my dearest love."

Jacinda's heart soared. He wanted to marry her out of love, not duty. No matter how dreadful the night had been, she couldn't contain her joy.

A gasp sounded behind them. They'd been so taken with one another they'd forgotten they were not alone.

"Do you mean to tell me that you aren't truly married?" Cousin Millie marched up beside them a martial light in her eyes.

Jacinda grinned sheepishly at her cousin. "It was a ruse. Mr. Wilkins and the captain thought a husband would—"

Cousin Millie raised her hands to her cheeks in dismay. "You have been in adjoining rooms for weeks now, do you not understand what that means? You are ruined, Jacinda." The lady paced back and forth. "I have failed your mother—"

"Miss Markham!" Drew put out a hand to halt her progress on one of her pacing passes. "If you will so kindly calm down, I was in the process of asking your niece to make it official. I love her to distraction and so I told her earlier."

The lady glared at him, then at Jacinda, who had eyes only for the captain. "That still doesn't keep everyone in the neighborhood from knowing that you two have been . . . well, living scandalously. After all, Captain, your reputation in Somerset is such as to make people—"

Jacinda slipped an arm round Millie's shoulders. "If you won't tell anyone, we won't. After this unfortunate business with Aunt Devere is straightened out, the captain and I"—she gazed at him with such passion it was all the gentleman could do not to take her in his arms right there in front of Millie—"will make it legal."

"A Special License is what is needed." Millie's chin settled into a stubborn jut.

The captain nodded. "Then a Special License it shall be. I shall leave as soon as possible and we will marry immediately on my return, if you, dear Cousin Millie, will discreetly acquire the services of a vicar."

The spinster's eyes brightened. "Leave everything to me."

Drew smiled at Jacinda, and nothing seemed to matter but the feel of his hand in hers. After a moment of silence, Cousin Millie looked from one face to the other then harrumphed. "You"—she took Jacinda's arm—"need a bath and treatment for that nasty burn. And you, sir"—she gestured for the captain to head for the door—"need to go help with the search and not stand in here mooning over my dear cousin."

Drew reached out and captured Jacinda's chin before Miss Markham was able to pull her away. He gave her a kiss that held a promise of more to come. "I shall see you later, my dear Jack."

Jacinda watched him step into the darkness while Millie chattered about having the parlor maids clean the tiny chapel for the wedding at Chettwood. It had never been used since the Blanchett family had come to the estate, but it would be perfect. The woman insisted it wouldn't do wed in Westbury and have all the neighbors learn about the *faux* marriage. Jacinda scarcely heard one word in three.

Near ten o'clock that evening, one of the grooms found the missing Mrs. Devere huddled in the carriage house out of the rain. The lady proved to be completely incoherent, babbling nonsense. By the time they got her to the manor, she'd fallen into stony silence, her expression vacant, and she didn't respond to anything or anyone, not even to Prudence, who begged her to speak. The doctor who'd been summoned had remained after treating both Ben and Jacinda's injuries. On seeing the blank-faced stare of the lady, he immediately ordered her to be taken to her room. Some twenty minutes later, he joined those waiting in the drawing room, leaving her in the care of a maid and her daughter.

Jacinda had bathed and was dressed in a simple pink gown, her hand neatly bandaged. Seated beside Drew, they rose when the doctor entered the room. "How is my aunt, sir?"

"Her condition is not good." He frowned, then sat his medical bag down to take the cup of tea Stritch offered him.

Mr. Blanchett, seated near the fireplace, shoved his own teacup away on the nearby table. "When can we speak with her? She has much to explain about her actions, albeit we've figured most of it out."

The doctor took a sip of tea, then said, "I don't think you will be able to question her."

"What do you mean, Doctor?" Drew asked. Like all the others, he wanted Mrs. Devere to confirm her involvement in Jacinda's father's death.

The physician stared into his tea cup a moment. "I fear the lady has gone quite mad. When she does speak, its only to rant incoherently and pull out her hair, then she falls silent again and doesn't respond to anything. It is very sad."

"Mad?" Mr. Wilkins seemed perplexed for a moment, putting aside the sandwich he had been enjoying, having missed his supper because of the search. "Do you mean she will have to be sent to an asylum?"

Dr. Fleetwood nodded. "It is the safest thing to do."

Jacinda's heart plummeted. While she agreed with Drew that her aunt had arranged her father's murder, she would have liked to have heard the truth from the lady. "Doctor, would it not be possible to keep her here at Chettwood, where she would be more comfortable?"

He set down his cup and took her hand. "My dear, the lady has shown a tendency to violence. You might still be in danger from her. From what I've observed, this type of madness sometimes leaves them with brief moments of seeming coherency . . . which makes them a danger to themselves and others. 'Tis my belief that it's better for the family if such members are put in a safer place, one equipped to deal with people so afflicted."

Drew slid an arm round Jacinda's waist. "Then Mrs. Devere must go somewhere else. I won't have you in danger. Doctor have you some place in mind?"

Jacinda started to protest when Doctor Fleetwood interrupted. "It's for the best, my dear. There's a physician down in Brighton who runs a very good asylum. He has done very good work helping the afflicted live close to normal lives. And very often when removed from the things that torture them the most, they improve."

Jacinda's distress was written on her face. At last she seemed to come to a decision. "If Prudence agrees, then so shall I."

Giles Devere, who'd been sitting sullenly in the corner, asked, "And what is to happen to Prudence and me? We cannot stay here after what Mama has done." More likely he couldn't stay because he owed money to most of the local gentlemen, but no one pointed that out.

Jacinda was perplexed as to how to handle things. She knew that Prudence would prefer to live near her mother, while Giles would live wherever someone provided him a home. But how could she afford it, now that the foundry had burned? "Mr. Wilkins, have

I the money to provide my cousins with a house near Brighton?"

The old gentleman cleared his throat. "Don't fret child. I shall make arrangements for the Deveres to live near their mother."

The doctor nodded. "You must keep the lady here for several days until I can write to Dr. Camden and make certain he can take her." He took his bag off the table, but, instead of going to the door, he turned back to Jacinda. "It would be best to keep the lady's door locked. She might have a tendency to wander during her animated moments, especially at night when she is alone." With that advice, he wished them good day and departed.

There was an uncomfortable silence for a moment. Mr. Blanchett, his face etched with fatigue, struggled out of his chair and came to Jacinda. "Don't let this business make you melancholy, child. This was your father's doing and we shall do what we can to make it right."

"Thank you, Uncle. I fear I have too much to do with the estate to allow myself to be blue deviled. I shall need the funds to provide for my family."

The gentleman shot a glance at Wilkins who, strangely, gave a nod of assent. "Well, that's not exactly true."

"What do you mean, sir?" Her gaze followed her uncle to Thomas Wilkins.

The solicitor crossed the room and in a low voice said, "Come to the library, my dear, there are some things we need to discuss in private."

Drew gave her hand an encouraging squeeze. "Go, I am acquainted with what the gentlemen have to say;

they informed me on first arriving and I agreed with the plan. I shall see if Ben has finally gone to sleep."

Jacinda's nerves were on edge as she follow the two older gentlemen to her library. She'd been through so much that day, she couldn't think what she was about to hear. Once there, Mr. Wilkins got to the point. "The foundry did burn my dear, but only a small portion was ruined. Your uncle should have it fully operational by the winter."

Seeing the bewildered expression on Jacinda's face, Mr. Blanchett took up the tale. "You see, Mr. Wilkins and I decided to paint a darker picture in the hopes of convincing whoever wanted your fortune there was nothing left worth killing for but the land."

The solicitor shrugged. "As I said before, we had it all wrong. If I'd have thought this silly plan would make someone attack you, I would never have tried it, my dear. It was intended to do the opposite. I just knew from the captain's letters that you were getting restless and perhaps a little reckless." He arched a brow at her.

Jacinda didn't want to think about the even more dangerous plan she'd concocted. She blinked in surprise. "I'm not penniless?"

"Not a bit, my dear." Uncle Matthew looked sheepishly at her. "We only did what we thought would help you."

"I know. I don't blame you." She tried to smile at him, but was too dazed and tired to do so properly.

Her uncle came up and hugged her. "If I am forgiven, then I shall return to London in the morning now that you are safe. Unless you want me to stay until your aunt is safely out of the manor."

"That won't be necessary, Uncle. I know how much you hate to leave the business."

"As to that, Claude is overseeing things." The old gentleman made a strangled noise in his throat. It was clear he didn't have much faith in his son's skills. "I shall go to bed so that I can get an early start." He turned to the solicitor. "Are you returning to London with me, Wilkins?"

"No, I shall stay at Chettwood a few days longer. There are estate matters that I must see to. Miss Blanchett and I must make arrangements for a house in Brighton before the Deveres move. Hopefully the doctor is wrong and we might get more answers from the woman than he thinks."

Uncle Matthew frowned. "Do you not think she was the one who hired those thugs so long ago?"

"I'm certain she did, but I would like to understand what she was thinking."

Jacinda sighed. "I'm not certain we shall ever know why."

Her uncle patted her shoulder. "Put it all behind you. Miss Markham tells me that you and the captain intend to make your marriage legal. Enjoy your life, my dear. Don't dwell on what's past. You deserve it after all you've been put through." He kissed her cheek and said good night.

After he left, Mr. Wilkins came round the desk and kissed Jacinda's cheek. "I, too, should like to wish you happy. Who would have thought it would all have ended in a love match? Delightful. In the morning I shall write my clerk to engage an agent to look for a property in Brighton once I have Dr. Camden's direction."

Jacinda smiled, but it slipped from her lips when guilt overcame her. How could she feel so wonderful when

Prudence and her family were devastated? "The captain wants to go for a Special License tomorrow and marry at once, but I think it not—"

"Don't delay, my dear child. Don't let anything stop you from being happy. Besides, I should like to be here for the ceremony if it is taking place in the next few days. I do so love a good wedding cake."

Despite herself, Jacinda laughed. "Then we shall have the wedding as soon as the captain can procure a license. I wouldn't want you to miss the celebration."

Mr. Blanchett and the captain left Chettwood some two hours apart the following morning. The elder gentleman departed at dawn, hoping to make London in time for his supper. Drew wanted to spend time with Jacinda, and since Mr. Wilkins had convinced him he only need go as far as Bath, where the bishop could issue the Special License he wanted because both he and Jacinda were from Somerset, he lingered until eight.

At his carriage, the captain pulled Jacinda into his arms. The embrace felt so right that she wasn't the least embarrassed that Mr. Wilkins and her cousin Millie watched from the front drawing room window. "I shall try to be back by tonight, or tomorrow morning at the latest. Promise me you'll stay close to the manor."

Her brow crinkled. "But I thought the danger was past. Everyone says so."

He brushed back a curl the wind tugged across her cheek. "True, but we might never know for certain unless your aunt's condition improves. I don't want you riding alone. I have asked Mr. Wilkins and Weems to watch out for you ladies. Promise me you won't stray far."

"But what about estate matters, I—"

"Nothing is so critical that it cannot wait until I return. I won't consider you completely safe until I have a ring on your finger."

Jacinda started to protest that she could take care of herself, but she knew that was foolish. If not for Drew she wouldn't be here enjoying life. Besides, he would be back in a day's time. "I promise. If Cousin Millie has her way, we will be in the chapel, which she swears has not seen a duster in twenty years."

Drew laughed and kissed her, then climbed into the carriage. He tipped his hat to the solicitor and Cousin Millie, who waved, then the captain drove away. Jacinda stayed on the drive and watched until his carriage disappeared from view. She was surprised by how much she already missed him. With a sigh she decided to go up and see how Ben was getting along.

The lad was restless and wanting out of bed, but Dr. Fleetwood had insisted that he remain quiet for the day. Jacinda extracted a promise that he would stay in his room by promising him two servings of cake after the wedding.

"You are marrying the captain." Ben's eyes shone.

Jacinda blushed. "I am."

"I knew he was a capital fellow." He scrambled from the bed to hug her but his knee reminded him he was hurt, so she came and hugged him. Giving him several books she'd gleaned from her father's collection, he settled down to enjoy the day as best as such an active boy could in bed.

Despite her cousin's desire for a discreet ceremony, the household was in a flutter of wedding preparations when she came downstairs. Cousin Millie had informed them of the news that a proper ceremony would be performed in the chapel, but not a word about it was to be mentioned outside the walls of Chettwood. Most being longtime servants, they asked no questions. They were only elated at the prospect of a family party that the lady had promised would include the servants. A Special License marriage it might be, but Miss Markham insisted they not stint on the arrangements. For Jacinda, all that mattered was that she and Drew would be together, so she allowed her cousin full reign.

The remainder of Jacinda's morning was spent with the parlor maids in the chapel, directing the cleaning, while Millie drove into Westbury to arrange for the vicar's services. Later, there was the menu for the wedding breakfast to be planned. Cook wanted to go all out, but Jacinda insisted it be simple. That evening after supper, when Mr. Wilkins could hardly keep his eyes open after the week's excitement and retired early, Jacinda and her cousin chose a gown from her new wardrobe for a wedding dress. It was a simple white silk gown worked with gold thread at the bodice, sleeves, and hem. The tulle overskirt was worked with tiny gold flowers.

Jacinda's only disappointment with the day was that Drew hadn't made it back before dark. As she finished undressing for bed a knock sounded on her door. Martha opened the door to Prudence, who looked as if she hadn't had a wink of sleep in two days. Neither she nor Giles had joined the family for meals all day and Jacinda hadn't objected. She knew they both had a great deal to comprehend. Prudence was clutching a small book, which Jacinda thought might be a bible.

Guilt resurfaced. Jacinda dismissed Martha as she asked her half-sister to come inside. All the fuss about her wedding had kept Jacinda from going to see how her aunt had been.

Prudence hesitated a moment, then said, "I came to apologize. I know now that everything you said about my mother last night was true."

"How is Aunt Devere?" It was strange but she had never referred to her aunt by her first name her entire life, preferring instead the more formal address.

Prudence shook her head. "I don't think she will ever speak again after the horrid things she's done. You may not think it, but I do assure you she has a conscience. I believe that was what drove her over the edge both today and so long ago."

Jacinda took her sister's hand and gave it a comforting squeeze. "I'm so sorry."

A ghost of a smile flitted over Prudence's pale face. She held out the book. "I've been reading the journal that she's kept all these years. At one point she thought herself in love with your father. It all went so very wrong when she discovered herself . . . with child. My father, that is . . . Mr. Devere . . . hadn't been home in months, so she knew the truth. She was forced to go to Town and see her husband to make him think I was his." Her voice grew shaky and Jacinda moved closer and put her arm around her sister.

Jacinda led Prudence to a sofa, where they sat in silence for a few minutes before Prudence continued. "After Devere died Mother applied to his brother, the viscount, for assistance, but he refused. He'd guessed the truth about Mama and Mr. Blanchett. She was forced to come here and ask for help and your mother insisted that they take us in. It's unclear whether Mrs. Blanchett knew the truth."

Jacinda wondered if her own mother had known that

the little red-haired girl had Blanchett blood in her veins. It made her proud to think her mother had been such a good woman, to take in someone who'd done her a wrong. She bit her lip a moment before she asked the sensitive question. "Does your mother mention my father's murder?"

Prudence put the book in Jacinda's lap. "If you read the journal, you can have little doubt that mother was behind the plot. By the time you were twelve, she hated your father excessively. She was livid when he started making arrangements for your 'grand marriage,' as she refers to it. It's a bit incoherent for a few days after she heard about his approaching Baron Rowland. There are threats and vows of vengeance. I'm sorry."

"*You* mustn't feel guilty. This is old history. You had nothing to do with what happened. You are as much a victim as I. I can only tell you that I'm delighted to have a sister, but if you prefer that we not tell the world, I shall understand."

Prudence's chin lifted, her eyes took on a defiant stare. "I don't give a fig what the world thinks." She leaned in and hugged Jacinda. "I must warn you that Giles is rather upset that this will get out. He is hoping to make an advantageous marriage and fears Mother's scandal will blight his chances."

It pained Jacinda to admit to herself that she didn't like Giles, but for Prudence's sake she would do what was best for her cousin. "Then we shall keep this among the family."

The ladies sat and talked for over an hour about what plans were being made for Mrs. Devere and for Prudence and Giles. At ten o'clock, Prudence excused herself, saying she intended to look in on her mother before she retired.

By the time Jacinda crawled into bed that evening, she'd gone a long way toward forming a bond with Prudence. As she closed her eyes to sleep she smiled, knowing she would see Drew on the morrow and that the whole world would be right.

CHAPTER NINE

A noise woke Jacinda a little after midnight. She sat up and listened. Had Drew returned home so late? Eager to see him, she slipped from bed and grabbed her wrapper. As she slid into the lace-trimmed garment, a door creaked down the hall. But it was in the opposite direction from Drew's room. Curious who would be up and about at this hour, she opened her door. The hallway was in darkness. Worried that her aunt might have taken a turn for the worse, she stepped back into her room and lit a candle. She would wake Prudence if Aunt Devere needed assistance, for it was clear that the lady wouldn't wish Jacinda's presence, even in her current state.

With the candleholder firmly in hand, she made her way down the hall. She rounded the corner and halted in surprise. Aunt Devere's door stood wide open. How could that be? Even the servants had been told it must be locked. Slowly Jacinda edged to the doorway. The lone candle's light barely penetrated the room. She stepped inside, making her way to her aunt's bed. She lifted the candle. The covers were tossed back and the bed was empty.

Worry filled her as she searched the four corners of the dark room. Her aunt was loose somewhere in the manor. It was frightening to think that the lady might try to do someone harm. Jacinda hurried into the hall, heading for her sister's room. She pounded on Prudence's door but got no response. About to open the door, a noise echoed down the hall, grabbing her attention. Thinking it might be the ladies, Jacinda moved toward the sound.

Even as she searched, her mind raced. Who had left the door unlocked? Prudence, Giles, or a servant? Out of the darkness a hand suddenly clamped over Jacinda's mouth as an arm crushed her against a masculine body. The candle flew from her hand and snuffed out when the holder clattered to the rug. In the darkness, the smell of leather, tobacco, and brandy filled her nose. She couldn't move.

A familiar voice growled in her ear. "I'll get my revenge, once and for all, and everyone will blame crazy Aunt Devere." A deep chuckle sounded. "And there's nothing you or your captain can do to stop me this time."

Before she could do anything, a sharp pain pierced her temple. In her mind she screamed Drew's name before she tumbled headlong into blackness.

Drew pushed his cattle down the dark road from Westbury. Thankfully, the moon was full and the road lay before him like a white ribbon on dark cloth. It had taken him until almost two o'clock that afternoon to track down the bishop in Bath. Then the clergy had insisted they return to his office for the proper documents and seals. Perhaps it was foolish, but he'd decided to return to Chettwood that very night. He couldn't wait to make Jacinda his bride. He didn't understand why, but he wouldn't feel his love was safe until he was able to give her his name without pretense.

The gates of Chettwood were a welcome sight. He drove his horses through and headed straight for the stables. Within ten minutes, he had the animals out of their traces and in stalls, having decided not to wake any of the grooms. He closed the stable doors and made his way to the house.

Drew patted his pocket with the ring he'd bought for Jacinda. A smile came to him. He would explain to her that his father had long ago sold the family betrothal ring, so he'd been forced to buy a new one. He had chosen a bold design of emeralds and diamonds that reminded him of her. He stepped into the rose garden and stopped. Movement caught his eye on the upper floor. The flickering of light played through the slit in the curtain. Who was up so late?

To his disbelief, the curtains suddenly burst into flames. Someone's room was on fire. In the darkness he couldn't tell which, but he had little doubt who was the target. Drew raced to the house and hammered on the locked door. It seemed like hours before a bleary-eyed footman unlocked the door but in fact it was only minutes.

Drew ran past him, shouting, "There's fire upstairs! Summon help!" He didn't wait to see what the footman did. He had to get to Jacinda's room. He threw open her door and stared at silent darkness.

"Jacinda?" He called to her but there was no answer. Her room wasn't on fire, but she wasn't in her bed. Fear twisted in his gut.

He ran down the hall looking for light under a doorway. He turned at the end of the hall and saw the soft glow of light on the hall rug. The smell of smoke was faint but distinct.

Drew ran full tilt and threw open the door. The curtain and bed hangings in the room were in flames. A pile of clothing burned in front of the wardrobe. To Drew's amazement, Thomas Wilkins lay in the bed, his nightcap covering one eye as he snored like a foghorn. Drew ran to the old gentleman and tried to wake him.

"Sir! Sir! Mr. Wilkins!" Drew shouted over the crackle of the flames. Still the old gentleman slept on. Drew spied a glass on the table and sniffed it.

Footsteps sounded in the hall. Stritch and the footmen appeared at the door with buckets of water. Drew shouted, "We must move him, I think he'd been drugged."

The men used their buckets of water on the curtains while the butler and Drew lifted the sleeping man and moved him into the hallway.

"Where is Miss Blanchett? She's not in her room."

Stritch shook his head. "I don't know, sir. She retired early with her cousin. I think it was something to do with choosing a wedding dress from her wardrobe."

Drew stared back into the room while the footmen struggled to contain the blaze. Someone intended to kill Mr. Wilkins. How easy would it have been to kill two birds with one stone? Drew stepped back into the room. It was only Wilkins's clothes smoldering now. Drew's gaze lifted to the closed wardrobe where the clothing had been stored. He kicked the pile aside and yanked open the door. Jacinda was stuffed inside, her hands and feet bound, a gag over her mouth. She leaned forward. He quickly undid the strip of cloth that bound her mouth.

"Thank God you found me."

He kissed her hard, then asked, "Who did this?"

"Weems." She said the man's name as if she couldn't comprehend such stunning news.

Drew stared a moment. "The steward? But why?"

She nodded her head. "I don't understand, but I intend to find out."

He lifted her out of the tiny space and carried her to her room. "No, my love, you are going to stay here while *I* go find him." Several thoughts of what he would do with the man played in his head. He lay her on her bed and worked on the binding round her hands and legs.

"I'm going with you. If that look in your eye means what I think—we won't learn anything if you kill him."

After the last rope came free, he kissed her forehead. "I want to but I shan't. I shall only capture him and hold him for the constable. Like you I want answers. Did he say anything?"

"Only that he'd gotten his revenge and they would blame Aunt Devere. Oh, great heavens, before he grabbed me I found Aunt Devere missing from her room. You don't think he harmed her, do you?"

"I think he was trying to kill you and Mr. Wilkins. He had drugged the old gentleman. As to your aunt, we have not seen her, so hopefully he merely released her."

Jacinda slid from the bed. "I must go and see how he is."

Drew protested she should stay in bed, but the determined look on her face meant she would go. He shrugged as followed her down the hall to the room where the servants had moved the solicitor. The old gentleman was just waking, befuddled by those who surrounded him. He was still too groggy to answer questions.

Prudence, in wrapper and nightcap, appeared in the doorway, her eyes heavy-lidded. "The noise and smell of smoke woke me. I fear I took some of the sleeping potion the doctor left. My mother is missing from her room." She glanced behind her at the smoke still lingering in the hall. "Tell me Mama is not responsible for what is happening?"

Jacinda went to her sister. "Not a bit of it, but I fear Weems has taken her somewhere. He did all this, intending to lay the blame at your mother's door."

"Weems?" Perplexed and a bit groggy, she could only shrug. "I don't understand."

Drew came to where the ladies stood. "Nor do we, madam, but I intend to find out." He moved past them into the hall.

"I'm coming with you." Jacinda stepped forward.

"Not in your bedclothes." He stepped back to her, giving her a light kiss. "You stay here with Mrs. Tyne and organize the search for her mother." Without further discussion, he strode down the hall.

Jacinda was torn as she watched him go. She'd waited so long for the truth, and now she was to be left behind.

Prudence was no fool. She tugged her sister down the hall. "Come, we shall dress and *I* shall handle the search for my mother. You go after the captain."

The two ladies disappeared in the direction of their own rooms.

Some fifteen minutes later Jacinda stopped by the gun room and found one of her father's dueling pistols. They were beautiful pieces that he often took out and showed his friends but to Jacinda's knowledge they had never been fired in anger. She hoped she wouldn't have to use them tonight.

The steward's cottage lay in complete darkness. Drew stood in the shadows of a large birch tree, watching the house. There was no movement or sound from the darkened windows.

A crackle of leaves behind him made him spin. Jacinda stepped to where he was waiting.

"I told you not to come." Despite his words he pulled her into his arms.

"I must hear the truth from his lips."

Drew stroked her hair. It wouldn't be fair to exclude her after all she'd suffered at this man's hands. "Very well, but stay in the background until I have him secured."

"I will." They moved back to watch the house in silence for a moment. After several minutes, Jacinda asked, "Do you think he's in there?"

"Without a doubt. It's part of his plan. He drugged Mr. Wilkins, stuffed you into that wardrobe, set the fire, then returned to the cottage to pretend he knows nothing. What he planned after that I cannot say." Anger raged inside him. He'd trusted the man. Why, he'd even asked the man to watch out for Jacinda.

No movement was visible at the windows. Drew signalled Jacinda to stay hidden, then moved to the front door and knocked. It was several moments before a light appeared in the windows. The door opened and Weems, in his nightcap, a lantern in his hand, appeared to have just gotten out of bed.

"Captain, what's wrong?"

He sounded so genuine Drew thought the man could tread the boards and rival the best talent on the stage. "Don't play the innocent, Weems. Your plan is finished. We saved Miss Blanchett and Wilkins from the fire unharmed. I shall see you hanged for your work this night."

The steward face twisted in frustration. He backed away from the angry glare in Drew's eyes. "I've waited eight years for my chance and you think you can come back and ruin it?"

Weems threw the lantern at Drew, but thankfully it didn't break until it hit the floor. The steward raced for the rear door, but he wasn't fast enough. The captain grabbed him and threw him back into the room. He crashed into a table, knocking a bottle of brandy to the floor. The liquid splattered onto the candle and the flame from the candle ignited the rug with surprising intensity. The steward regained his balance and came at Drew, fists flying. The man had no formal training, but what he lacked in skill he made up for in strength. His first jab clipped Drew's shoulder, knocking him backward into a table, which shattered. Taking advantage of the moment, Weems ran at the open front door, disappearing into the darkness.

Drew hastened to his feet and went after the villian but he didn't have far to go. Weems had run headlong into Stritch, who had arrived armed and had been knocked down by the fleeing steward. The two men struggled on the ground until Drew put his foot on Weems's arm, pinning him down. Then he helped the old butler rise.

"Are you all right, Stritch?"

The old man was short of breath, but he straightened his robe and said, "In fine curl, sir, now that we've got this blackguard."

Jacinda appeared out of the darkness. She glared down at the man who'd changed her life so long ago, but could find no words to say to him. Instead, she stepped back as Drew and Stritch pulled the steward to his feet and dragged him back to the cottage. Drew shoved him in a chair. The fire on the rug had gotten a good hold and much of the material was ablaze. Stritch went toward it to put it out, but Drew stopped him.

"Stritch, find me some rope, instead." Drew never took his gaze from the steward, who sat in the chair gasping for air after his mad dash and mill with the butler. He glared at Jacinda who stood mutely in the doorway watching him.

The old servant handed the ancient pistol to the captain then began to search the room, staying away from the ever-growing blaze. Within minutes he found short lengths of rope in a chest near the door. He held them up for Drew and a knowing look passed between the men.

While Stritch tied the man to the chair, Drew asked the most pressing question. "Where is Mrs. Devere? Is she here?"

The steward's face became a stone mask of indifference. This wasn't going to be easy.

"Weems," Drew leaned close as the butler finished his task and stepped back. "Either you talk and tell us what we want to know or," Drew straightened and looked at the fire which had spread from the rug up the leg of a chair, "we leave you to the fate that you intended for Miss Blanchett and Wilkins." It was a bluff. No matter what the man had done, Drew wouldn't do such a thing, but he hoped such a man wouldn't see though the threat. He looked at Jacinda and for a moment horror filled her eyes, then she saw the truth in his face. After an almost imperceptible nod she remained silent, allowing him to handle the man.

Weems eyes grew wide as he watched the fire spread. "You—you can't."

"I can and I will. Where is Mrs. Devere?"

"I—I only woke her up and took her outdoors. She's somewhere in the gardens. I thought since she'd tried to burn her niece once, that it would be the perfect opportunity to cover what I did."

Relief filled Drew. He'd been afraid the man had done something more to the old woman. His brow flattened. "Why are you trying to kill Miss Blanchett? There can be little doubt you arranged her father's murder. What is this about?"

Weems's face twisted with painful memories and he yelled at Jacinda. "Your father deserved to die. I wanted him to suffer the way I suffered for his dastardly behavior."

Her hand moved to her throat. The hatred in his voice was chilling. "My father wronged you?"

"The scoundrel ruined my only sister, a beautiful young girl in the prime of her youth. She was but seventeen when he met her in Bath and . . . and took her virtue by making her think he loved her. It was only later she learned he was married with a wife and child of his own. Within a month she learned she was with child." Weems grew quiet for a moment, staring into the flames on the floor, tears rolling down his face. "She threw herself into the Avon rather than bear the shame. When they pulled her body from the river I swore I'd make him pay." A satisfied calm came to his face. "And I did."

"But why kill Jacinda? She was an innocent in all that." Drew believed the man was almost as mad as Mrs. Devere. His quest had consumed his whole life.

Weems's gaze raked Jacinda with disdain. "Why should she live when my sister lies cold in her grave?"

"And Wilkins? Why murder him?"

A cunning grin curled the corners of the man's mouth. "The parlor maids were always nattering about what the Quality were doin'. I found out everyone had been looking for a new will that was drawn up just be-

fore he died. So I went to Bath and found a man who
drew up a will that left the foundry fortune to Giles Devere and the estate to me. It was dated the last week of
Blanchett's life. Wilkins would have been one of the few
people who might have questioned the signature or the
contents."

Drew and Jacinda exchanged a surprised look. Neither expected a conspiracy. "Giles was in this with
you?"

Weems gave a superior laugh. "I'd hardly throw my
lot in with that fool, but he makes a perfect sacrifice,
does he not? Always in need of money for his gamin',
expensive tastes, and without many redeemin' features.
Admit it, you all suspected him, did you not?"

Drew couldn't deny he was right. "But don't you
think everyone would have questioned leaving an estate
to a man who was a complete stranger when there were
family survivors?"

"I can run this estate far better than any member of
Blanchett's family. The man had littered the countryside
with his by-blows. I merely wrote a letter pretending my
mother had declared me to be the man's son. After the
fire I meant to stash the letter and the will in a secret
panel in the desk in the library. I saw him open it once
when he didn't know I was watching. I searched it after
he died and the girl disappeared. It has a list of his dirty
little mistakes and the payments made to cover himself."

Sickened, Jacinda turned her back on Weems to stare
out into the darkness. It was clear that her father's deeds
and their aftermath were causing her great pain. But she
wasn't so weak she would give up before she'd heard the
whole story. With her back still to him she asked, "And
who were those men who attacked us?"

"My cousin and his friend did the deed for a mere ten

pounds and passage to America, so the law can't get their hands on them," Weems gloated.

Drew wanted to smash the man's face but he held himself in check. "And who fired the shot at Jacinda on her first day back."

The steward pressed his lips closed, but when Drew pulled him towards the burning rug, he began to speak, "A man I met in an ale house in Wells. I hired him when I learned she"—he gestured at Jacinda with his head—"was comin' home. He'd lost a leg in the war and couldn't find work. Claimed he was a marksman, but he missed."

"I want his name." Drew demanded.

"Crawley's his name. But he's gone back to London, so you'll never find him."

"No, but a magistrate might." A small clock on the mantelpiece chimed the hour of two. There would be nothing more accomplished tonight. "Stritch, we must take Weems back to the manor. Is there some place we can lock him up until morning?"

"The cellars, sir."

Drew moved to take Jacinda in his arms while Stritch undid the man's ropes. "Have you heard what you came to hear?"

She nodded her head, her gaze on the brandy-induced fire. As she looked at the shards of glass, it struck her that the brandy was from her father's private stock—but none of that mattered now. "We must do something or the cottage will burn."

Drew went into the small bedroom. He came back with a blanket, which he threw over the fire, then stamped on the flames beneath. It smoldered and the flames, unrestrained for so long, resisted his efforts.

All eyes were on the process. Weems suddenly darted

for the door. But instead of escaping, he grabbed Jacinda in a stranglehold.

Drew stepped toward him but stopped as Weems's arm tightened round her neck. "I'll kill her if you come closer."

"Let her go." Drew demanded even as his gut clenched. He couldn't lose Jacinda now. They would be able to live at last out from under the cloud of fear that had dogged her for eight years.

Weems backed towards the door, pulling her with him. "I may not get the estate, but I shall certainly avenge my sister's—"

A dull thud sounded as the man stiffened, his eyes rolled up in his head and he groaned. His arm slid from Jacinda as he collapsed to the ground. She ran straight into Drew's open arms. There in the doorway stood Thomas Wilkins in his nightshirt and banyan, a piece of firewood in his hand.

"Burn my best jackets, will you?" He glared down at Weems body as Drew pulled Jacinda into his arms. "What the devil was this man's game?" The old solicitor looked from Stritch to Drew to Jacinda.

The captain sighed. "It's a long, ugly story and I shall tell it all in the morning. Stritch, remain here and keep a guard on Weems. I shall take Miss Blanchett back to the house. We'll send James down to help take him to the wine cellar."

The old solicitor looked at the others for an explanation of what had happened, but Drew shook his head, signifying that it wasn't the time. Wilkins nodded. "I shall remain here with Stritch. Wouldn't want this dastard to come to and cause trouble again."

At a quarter past two o'clock, fatigue was evident in

all their faces. Still Jacinda asked, "What about Aunt Devere?"

Mr. Wilkins sat heavily on the chair recently vacated by the steward, the drug he'd been given still making him sluggish. "I quite forgot. That was why I came down. She was found wandering in the back meadow, perfectly unharmed."

Jacinda sagged into Drew's arm with relief, then her gaze roved to the man unconscious on the ground. Pain played on her face for the man she'd thought her friend. Drew squeezed her closer and she looked up at him.

"Come, my dear, you need to rest."

She didn't protest and allowed him to lead her out of the smoky cottage. She was so silent on the walk back that he became concerned. On the front steps of the manor, Drew stopped before he opened the door. "I adore you, my love. It's truly over at last and I want you to put all this behind you. Will you marry me tomorrow? We shall start anew."

He couldn't see her features in the darkness, but her voice sounded tired and defeated. "I feel so ashamed of what my father did. How much pain and hurt he caused. How can I just go on as if none of it matters?"

"Your father paid for his actions with his life and almost cost you yours. I cannot make my father any different from what he is—a gambler who will go straight back to his old ways the moment he is back on his feet. He is what he is as was your father. We, neither of us, must spend the rest of our lives trying to make up for their failings."

He heard her soft sigh, then she melted into his arms. "I do so love you."

Drew crushed her to him. "Then be mine. Sail to India with me. Once there I can arrange with my business partners to move my routes back to England. I'll sail the *Flying Dragon* in the Irish Seas instead. We can settle down here at Chettwood."

"India?" He heard the interest in her voice, then she said, "But I have been away for so long, shouldn't I—"

"Millie has done a wonderful job of seeing to things. Perhaps she would agree to continue for a while longer."

"But what about Ben?"

"Shall we take the scamp with us? We can hire a tutor to go as well."

She laughed. "He would certainly prefer it to school in the fall."

"Then say yes, my love." He could think of nothing better than sailing the seas with Jacinda. She would make his life complete.

"Yes, my love. A sea voyage would be just the thing for a new beginning," she whispered just before his lips covered hers.

More Regency Romance
From Zebra